A FRESH LOAF OF POETRY FROM JAPAN

Naoshi Koriyama
With an Introduction by Bruce Allen

CONTENTS

Acknowledgments... ix

Introduction   Bruce Allen   xii

Preface   Naoshi Koriyama   xv

SECTION 1

    A LOAF OF POETRY 1
    BRING HIM A BRUSH... 2
    UNFOLDING BUD 3
    TO A POET... 4
    LIKE A MILKMAID 4
    AN AUTUMN SONG 5
    A TRANSLATOR'S MORNING RITUAL 6
    A NAMELESS PROFESSOR MAKES UP HIS MIND 7
    POET AS A BAKER 7
    AT THIS TIME IN HISTORY 8
    TO AN INACTIVE, SILENT POET........................... 9
    MY FINGERS BEGIN TO DANCE 10
    TRIBUTE TO THE USED RIBBON 11
    WHITMAN BRISKLY STRODE 12
    WHITMAN'S BROADWAY.................................... 13
    DID HE SEE? 14
    UNDER YOUR KIND, FRIENDLY EYES 15
    TO P. M 16
    TO AN ENGLISH TEACHER IN JAPAN 17
    A GREAT TEACHER OF ENGLISH LITERATURE..... 18
    JANE TRINKLE READS MY POETRY ALOUD 19
    POETRY CLASS IN JAPAN.................................... 20
    ADVICE TO A POET 21

SECTION 2

- CAVE MAN'S MOONRISE 22
- THE AUGUST MOON 23
- THE MID-AUTUMN FULL MOON 24
- THE NEW MOON 25
- THE FULL MOON 26
- LET THE ADVANCED ASTRONOMER LOOK 26
- DISCOVERY OF A NEW PLANET 27
- LOOKING AT VENUS 28
- TIME AND SPACE 29
- A CAPTAIN'S MONOLOGUE 30
- TWO UNIVERSES 31
- ETERNAL GRANDEUR 32
- THE ROCK AT THE EDGE OF THE TALLEST HILL 33
- ON HIS GRANDMA'S ISLAND 34
- THE RAGING SEA IN A TYPHOON 35
- EARTH DAY 1990 36
- REMINISCENCE 37
- SUMMER ON THE HOME ISLAND 38
- HARVEST 39
- A THOUGHT BY A MOUNTAIN STREAM 40
- A VIEW OF EXPO '70 JUST BEFORE CLOSING 41
- KINKAKUJI TEMPLE 42
- BY THE LAKESHORE 43
- LAKE OHNUMA 44
- AT THE WONDERFUL CALL 45
- A BUSH WARBLER CALLED 46
- ON THIS SPRING DAY 47
- TO THE SWAN 48
- LET THE FISH HAPPILY SWIM 49
- A GARDENER 50
- CHESTNUTS ARE FULL AND RIPE 51
- ON THE EVENING OF APRIL 6, 2001 52
- LOVELIEST OF TREES, THE CHERRY NOW 53
- SWEETEST-SCENTED OF BLOSSOMS 54
- MYSTERIOUS IS THE UNIVERSE 55
- THE MOON IS BEAUTIFUL TONIGHT 56

SECTION 3

- TO THE PERSIMMON TREE 57
- THE EARTH RIPENS 58
- ON THIS FINE AUTUMN MORNING 59
- THE PERSIMMON TREE 60
- I GO OUT INTO THE YARD 61
- WINDLESS WOOD 62
- ESSENCE OF MORNING 63
- THROUGH THE WINDOW 64
- LET ME SEE YOUR BEAUTY 65
- WALK SLOWLY 66
- SEA TURTLE HATCHLINGS 67
- SO INNOCENT, SO BUSY 68
- TWO PENGUIN CHICKS 69
- THE GENTLE-EYED HIGHLAND BULL 70
- THE SUNSET 71
- AN IMAGE OF A HORSE 72
- KIKAI ISLAND OF AMAMI IN SOUTHERN JAPAN 73
- A TOMB ON AN OKINAWAN HILL 74
- MAN AGAINST NATURE 75
- A RAINBOW IN THE SKY 76
- OIL CRISIS 77
- KINGLY MOUNTAIN 78
- MT. SAKURAJIMA PUTS ON A SHOW 79
- THE BRIGHTEST MOON ABOVE MT. SAKURAJIMA 80
- LOOKING UP AT MT. FUJI 81
- BEHOLDING MT. FUJI 82
- THE EAGLE IN CAPTIVITY 83
- THE EAGLE IN THE CAGE 84
- HYMN TO THE GRAND CANYON 85
- GRAND CANYON IN THE SUN 86
- LOOKING OVER THE GRAND CANYON 87

SECTION 4

- AT A GARDEN IN KYOTO 88
- PROFESSOR PERRY D. WESTBROOK 89
- YOU DON'T KNOW HOW MUCH I OWE YOU 90
- ALL THE POEMS I HAVE WRITTEN I OWE YOU 91

A POEM FOR MRS. KENKICHI MASAI	92
TO AN ASTRONOMY PROFESSOR	93
THE BEAUTY OF OLD JAPANESE TALES	94
MY SCALPEL IS SHARP	95
TO ROBINSON JEFFERS	96
AT CARMEL IN THE SUMMER OF 1981	97
ON READING "SUMMER'S ARRIVAL" BY LINDA C. GRAZULIS	98
MY WIFE'S COUSIN WAS A NAVY PILOT	99
A HOUSE-DOG'S MONOLOGUE	100
A POET TALKING TO HIMSELF	101
A LITTLE GIRL	102
THIS SILENT NIGHT	103
PLAYING "DONAUWELLEN WALZER" ON THE ORGAN	104
MY GRANDFATHER	105
GRAVITATION	106
ONE MONTH OLD DAUGHTER	107
EXPLORATION	108
MY SECRETARY	109
SMALL GIRL AND UNIVERSE I, II	110
TONIGHT HE IS FIVE	112
AT THE END OF SUMMER HOLIDAYS	113
MY ART DEALER	114
IN AN ART MUSEUM	115
ALOHA OE	116
A MAN WHO DIDN'T BECOME A JUDO CHAMPION	117
THE WORLD CONGRESS OF POETS IN MILAN	118
A POEM WRITTEN IN MEMPHIS	119
EFFICIENT IMPRESARIO	120
AN AMAMI ISLAND FOLK SINGER	122
EASTERN AND WESTERN SHORES OF THE ISLAND	123
POETRY IS A MAGIC WAVE	124
POWER OF A SMALL ISLAND'S INDIGENOUS LANGUAGE	125
TO A YOUNG LADY	126
TO A COUSIN ON THE ISLAND	127
AT THE CONCERT HALL	128
A LOVE SONG JUST FOR YOU	129
A MORNING SONG	130
TO MY YOUNG GODDESS	131

ABOARD AN OCEAN LINER 132
A HYMN TO MY LADY 133
AN ARTIST'S APOLOGY TO HIS DAUGHTER 134
FANTASIA EROTICA 135
6.8 BILLION HUMAN BEINGS PRAYED FOR YOU 136
THE MOST WONDERFUL EVENING IN MY LIFE 137
ON THE GREAT WALL OF CHINA 138
AT AGE FOUR SCORE YEARS AND ELEVEN 139
130TH ANNIVERSARY OF TOYO UNIVERSITY 141

SECTION 5

JETLINER 144
LIKE A STATELY GIANT EAGLE 145
A JET LANDING IN CLOUDS 146
JETLINER UP IN THE STRATSPHERE 147
SONG OF A JET PILOT 148
THE PLANE'S SHADOW 149
SONG OF A LOCAL AIRLINE'S PILOT 150
I FEEL LIKE AN ASTRONAUT 151
THE LAST MINUTE CHECK 152
A GLIMPSE OF THE BRIDGE 153

SECTION 6

ONE OF THE MOST POWERFUL EARTHQUAKES 154
HUMANS ARE HELPLESS AGAINST NATURE'S POWER 155
THE INCREDIBLE POWER OF THE TSUNAMI 156
WHEN HUMANS ARE IN A CRISIS 157
ONE WEEK AGO TODAY 158
HOW WONDERFUL IT IS JUST TO BE ALIVE! 159

SECTION 7

I COULD GO STRAIGHT HOME 160
OF COURSE I WANT TO SING A SONG 161
THE SUN SAYS TO MAN 162
A NUCLEAR LEGEND 163
NUCLEAR WINTER 164
CIVILIZATION ADVANCES 165
THE PERSIAN CORMORANT IN PROTEST 166

NOTHING IS MORE PRECIOUS THAN PEACE 167
BRITISH TROOPS LEAVING SOUTHAMPTON....................... 168
TROOPS LEAVING ABOARD QUEEN ELIZABETH II 169
REQUIEM TO THE ISLAND HORSES 170
ARMAGEDDON AT OUR DOOR 171
CONFUSION 174

SECTION 8

A NEW YEAR SONG OF THE HORSE (1990) 175
A NEW YEAR SONG OF THE SHEEP (1991) 176
A NEW YEAR SONG OF THE MONKEY (1992)....................... 177
A NEW YEAR SONG OF THE ROOSTER (1993) 178
A NEW YEAR SONG OF THE DOG (1994) 179
A 14-LINE POEM OF THE WILD BOAR 180
A NEW YEAR SONG OF THE RAT (1996) 181
A NEW YEAR SONG OF THE COW (1997)............................. 182
A NEW YEAR SONG OF THE TIGER (1998) 183
A NEW YEAR SONG OF THE HARE (1999) 184
A NEW YEAR SONG OF THE DRAGON (2000)....................... 185
A NEW YEAR SONG OF THE SNAKE (2001) 187
A NEW YEAR SONG OF THE HORSE (2002) 188
A NEW YEAR SONG OF THE SHEEP (2003) 189
A NEW YEAR SONG OF THE MONKEY (2004)....................... 190
A NEW YEAR SONG OF THE ROOSTER (2005) 191
A NEW YEAR SONG OF THE DOG (2006) 192
A NEW YEAR SONG OF THE WILD BOAR (2007) 193
A NEW YEAR SONG OF THE RAT (2008) 194
A NEW YEAR SONG OF THE COW (2009)............................. 195
A NEW YEAR SONG OF THE TIGER (2010) 196
THE TIGER'S ADVICE TO MAN 197
A NEW YEAR SONG OF THE RABBIT (2011)......................... 198
A NEW YEAR SONG OF THE DRAGON (2012)....................... 199
A NEW YEAR SONG OF THE SNAKE (2013) 200
A NEW YEAR SONG OF THE HORSE (2014) 201
A NEW YEAR SONG OF THE SHEEP (2015) 202
A NEW YEAR SONG OF THE MONKEY (2016)....................... 203
A NEW YEAR SONG OF THE ROOSTER (2017) 204
A NEW YEAR SONG OF THE DOG(2018) 205

SECTION 9

- CHAUCER ABOARD A SPACESHIP 206
- CHAUCER AT CAPE KENNEDY 207
- CHAUCER ENJOYS *RICHARD III* IN TOKYO 208
- CHAUCER AT LEICESTER SQUARE 209
- CHAUCER AT THE 50TH REUNION 210

SECTION 10

- Poems translated into other languages 211
- Chinese: "My Grandfather" 211
- French: "Tankas" 212
- Greek: "Poetry Class in Japan" 214
- Italian: "At a Garden in Kyoto" 215
- Korean: "Time and Space" 216
  - "An Artist's Apology to his Daughter" 217
- Vietnamese: "A Loaf of Poetry" 218

About the Author 219

Publications 220

Poems Reprinted in School Textbooks 221

Acknowledgments

The following poems have previously appeared in the publications specified below. Grateful acknowledgments are made to the editors of these publications. The poems which have previously appeared in *The Christian Science Monitor* are copyrighted by *The Christian Science Monitor* and the poems are reprinted with permission of *The Christian Science Monitor*, for which I am grateful.

THE CHRISTIAN SCIENCE MONITOR
Unfolding Bud, (July 13,© 1957); Tribute to the Used Ribbon, (Dec. 20, ©1958); Poetry Class in Japan, (July19, ©1958) ; Cave Man's Moonrise, (July 27, © 1954); Harvest, (July 9, © 1958); The Kinkaku-ji Temple, (Dec. 26, © 1967); By the Lakeshore, (Jan. 3, © 1968); To the Persimmon Tree, (Feb. 25, © 1958); Windless Wood, (April 25, © 1955); Essence of Morning, (Oct. 8, © 1955); Through the Window, (March 21, ©1955); Kingly Mountain, (May 26, ©)1955); Mt. Sakurajima Puts on a Show, (Dec.12, ©1955); Looking up at Mt. Fuji, (June 11, ©1957); Gravitation, (Dec. 20, © 1955); Small Girl and Universe I, II, (April 1, © 1957); To a Young Lady, (June 25, © 1958)

THE ENGLISH JOURNAL
To P. M. on reading a commentary by P.M. on Hopkins' "Spring"

THE NEW YORK HERALD TRIBUNE
Bring Him a Brush; To a Poet

POETRY NIPPON
At This Time in History; To an English Teacher in Japan; A Captain's Monologue; Eternal Grandeur; On His Grandma's Island; A Tomb on an Okinawan Hill; Man against Nature; Oil Crisis; At a Garden in Kyoto; To an Astronomy Professor; My Grandfather; At the End of Summer Holidays; In an Art Museum; Fantasia Erotica; Jetliner; Requiem to the Island Horses; Chaucer aboard a Spaceship; Chaucer Enjoys *Richard III* in Tokyo

THE MAINICHI DAILY NEWS
Time and Space; Beholding Mt. Fuji; A House Dog's Monologue; Like a Stately Giant Eagle; A Jet Landing in Clouds; Nothing Is More Precious than Peace; British Troops

Leaving Southampton; Troops Leaving aboard Queen Elizabeth II; Armageddon at our Door; Chaucer at Leicester Square

POEMS OF THE WORLD
A Translator's Morning Ritual; Poet as a Baker; To an Inactive, Silent Poet; My Fingers Begin to Dance; Let the Advanced Astronomer Look; Discovery of a New Planet; At the Wonderful Call; A Bush Warbler Called; Let the Fish Happily Swim; On the Evening of April 6, 2001; Loveliest of Trees, the Cherry Now; Sweetest-Scented Blossoms; On This Fine Autumn Morning; The Persimmon Tree; I Go out into the Yard; Sea Turtle Hatchlings; My Art Dealer; Aloha Oe; An Amami Island Folk Singer; Eastern and Western Shores of the Island; A Love Song Just for You; I Feel like an Astronaut; A Song of the Dragon(2000); A New Year Song of the Snake(2001); A New Year Song of the Horse(2002); A New Year Song of the Cow (2009); A New Year Song of the Tiger (2010); The Tiger's Advice to Man: A New Song of the Rabbit (2011); A New Song of the Dragon (2012); A New Year Song of the Snake (2013); A New Year Song of the Horse (2014); A New Year Song of the Sheep (2015); A New Year Song of the Monkey (2016); A New Year Song of the Rooster(2017); My Wife's Cousin Was a Navy Pilot; Poetry Is a Magic Wave; At Age Four Score Years and Eleven

BRIDGING THE WATERS
An Artist's Apology to His Daughter, both in English and Korean

POETRY READING CIRCLE OF TOKYO ANTHOLOGY
The Most Wonderful Evening in my Life; The Rock at the Edge of the Tallest Hill; Of Course I Want to Sing a Song; The Gentle-Eyed Highland Bull; Kikai Island of Amami in Southern Japan; Hymn to the Grand Canyon; My Scalpel Is Sharp

THE ALBUM OF INTERNATIONAL POETS
A Loaf of Poetry

THE POET
The Full Moon; To the Swan; Father to Son

DECAL POETRY REVIEW
Reminiscence; A Thought by a Mountain Stream

CALAMUS: WALT WHITMAN QUARTERLY INTERNATIONAL
Did He See?; Whitman's Broadway; Whitman Briskly Strode

CIRRUS
Tankas du japon

As for the translations of my poems in other languages in SECTION 10, my deep gratitude is extended to the translators, publications, and editors. The Chinese translation of "My Grandfather" is posted on the Internet by Dr. Zhang Zhi; two French translations of tankas translated by Maxianne Berger are reprinted from *Cirrus, tanka de nos jours*; the Greek translation of "Poetry Class in Japan" by Zacharoula Gaitanaki is reprinted from the Greek publication provided by her; the Italian translation of "At a Garden in Kyoto" is reprinted from *Poesie* published in Italy in 1990; the Korean translation of "Time and Space" is sent by Jung-Kee Lee; the Korean translation of "An Artist's Apology to his Daughter" by Rachel S. Rhee & Kyung Hwa Rhee is reprinted from *Bridging the Waters* (Co-published by Korean Expatriate Literature & Cross-Cultural Communications, 2013); the Vietnamese translation of "A Loaf of Poetry" is posted on the Internet by a group of Vietnamese.

As for the illustrations, *Poems of the World* has granted me permission to use the following illustrations which have appeared in its previous issues. The list of the illustrations used is as follows:

An illustration of "a bird's eggs" (p. 36, Vol. 16 #4); "a dog" (p.32, Vol. 4 #4); "a sea turtle hatchling" (p. 9, Vol. 16 #4); "a dragon" (p. 35, Vol. 16 #2); "a horse" (p. 7, Vol. 6 #2); "a sheep" (p. 37, Vol. 19 #2) "fishes and birds" (p. 25, Vol. 20 #4); "a rooster" (p.16, Vol. 21 #2); "a rabbit" (p. 22, Vol. 15 #2); " a tiger" (p. 35, Vol. 14 #3)

Introduction

Naoshi Koriyama's poems in *A Fresh Loaf of Poetry* from Japan span the experiences and imagination of a long and intensely active life. They reflect and express the sweeping changes that have occurred during this time in Japan, in the world, and in his own personal life.

Naoshi Koriyama was born and raised in the rural beauty of the Amami Islands that lie between Okinawa and the main Japanese islands in 1926. The love and delight of nature that he discovered in childhood has remained an underlying presence throughout all his work. As he grew up, however, the peaceful life of his childhood was uprooted by the press of the world events that surrounded the Second World War. His struggles with issues of war and peace and his yearning to establish bonds of friendship among all peoples emerged as another central element in his work. In the difficult post-war period, he responded by going to the United States for university study. In this new land he overcame cultural, racial, and linguistic barriers. He made friends, mastered a foreign language, and became enthralled by the world of poetry. There, he learned the art of writing of poetry in this new tongue. Later, he returned to Japan, where he has continued to write and teach with unwavering zeal to encourage those in his own country to live up to its commitments to peace and international cooperation.

Naoshi Koriyama's poetry brings together his dedication to explore the poetic imagination with his moral fervor for conveying difficult truths to the world—a world that extends far beyond the confines of literary specialists. His poetry strikes inward, while at the same time it strikes outward. In a time when some poetry may appear hermetic and inward-looking to the point of losing wider audiences, his poems speak to a wide range of people; worldwide, and on many levels. What the Japanese call the *kotodama*—the spirit of words—is nurtured by the words of his poems.

As a teacher, I have seen Naoshi Koriyama's poems light up the faces and imaginations of students in university classes—including those of many who have previously been wary of the mysteries of poetry. His poems employ all the rich elements of literature; its metaphors, symbols, ambiguity, paradox, humor, irony; elements that can often frighten away those unfamiliar with poetry. Yet his poems also have the ability to unfold and awaken within readers the spirit that lies within them. In this regard I think particularly of his two poems "Unfolding Bud" and "A Loaf of Poetry". Students who had at first been baffled by the thoughts of metaphors, rhythms, and paradoxes have found that these poems release within them the metaphors they contain; like unfolding buds. They come to bake the spirit of the poems in the hearts of their own imaginations. It is thus fitting that he has chosen the title *A Fresh Loaf of Poetry* from Japan as the title of this collection.

In a time when some poets shy away from appearing too direct or didactic in expressing political, moral, and activist concerns, Naoshi Koriyama remains resolute in calling for writers and readers to wake up to the harsh realities our world is wrapped up in—the injustice, racism, greed, destruction of the earth, and the wars that threaten the existence of not only poetry but of all life. Poems like "At This Time in History" and "To an Inactive, Silent Poet" remind poets and readers alike of our responsibilities to get outside of our limited personal and poetic existences and to engage ourselves in the wider world as active, moral beings. He joins other socially committed poets in showing that poetry can be at the same time poetic and political, metaphorical and moral, specific and spiritual, and grounded and sublime.

I would also like to highlight Naoshi Koriyama's extensive work in translation; a joy and dedication that he celebrates in poems such as "A Translator's Morning Ritual". One aspect of his translation work includes the translation of his own poetry into English—although I suspect that he usually writes directly in English, without consciously "translating" from Japanese. Yet the very act of writing poetry can also be seen as a creative act of translating; translating from the *kotodama* that lies before and beyond the realm of written words. He has also patiently translated the work of numerous Japanese poets and writers-ranging from that of medieval Japanese tales to the modern work of Miyazawa Kenji and that of contemporary Japanese writers on war and peace and the Fukushima 3/11 tragedy. Several years ago I had the pleasure of working with him in translating ninety tales from the medieval collection *Konjaku monogatari shu*; a work that shows the striving of common people in Japan a thousand years ago to make peace with the land, with the soul, and with all beings. His long contribution to translation has communicated to people in other countries the power of the voices within Japan that have been calling out to the rest of the world to share in the spirit needed to stop war and to find peace among all humans, and other beings and places of the earth.

Naoshi Koriyama's present collection, *A Fresh Loaf of Poetry* from Japan, brings together many of the important poems of his long career. They express his ongoing love affair with words, people, and the world. It is inspiring to see in this collection the steady development of his art and his ongoing contributions to seeking a world of poetic imagination, freedom, and peace. It is my pleasure to help celebrate this work and encourage the continuance of its finding a place in the hearts of readers in the future.

Bruce Allen
Professor, Department of English Language and Literature
Seisen University
Tokyo, Japan

Preface

Since my poetry has been produced out of my life, I would like to write about my life history, rather than my poetry itself. Poems will speak for themselves. I was born on an island named "Kikaijima" in the Amami Islands that lie between mainland Japan and Okinawa in 1926. It's a small island roughly 30 miles around and its highest mountain is about 700 feet high. After finishing 8 years of elementary school education on the island, I went on to Kagoshima Normal School in mainland Japan in April 1941 at age 15. We had three hours of English a week in the first year. In December 1941, Japan started a war against the U.S.A. and Britain by attacking Pearl Harbor and Singapore. In the second year we had two hours of English a week, since the educational policy of the country was leaning toward discouraging English education, because English was the enemy's language. But our English teacher, Mr. Sanenori Kirihara, told us in our second year English class, "If we win the war, you will have your school trip to New York, and you will need your English there. If we lose the war, occupation forces will come over from the United States, and you will need your English. Either way, English will be very valuable to you, don't you think?" And I thought he was right, and I kept on studying English as much as I could by myself. In the third year and on, English was no longer taught at our school.

In 1945, I was in my fifth year at the Normal School, and I was drafted into the Army on June 10 and was sent to the southern part of mainland Japan, getting ready for a possible landing by the U.S. forces. The war came to an end on August 15, 1945. After the end of the war, I returned to my home island which I hadn't visited for two and a half years, because U.S. submarines had controlled the East China Sea. We, a group of people, who were born on Kikaijima chartered a small wooden fishing boat at a fishing town named Yamagawa, at the tip of the Satsuma Peninsula and returned to Kikaijima. There were no regular passenger boat services available between the Amami Islands and mainland Japan toward and after the end of the war. As there was an air base on Kikaijima, from which a total of about 100 Kamikaze special attack planes took off to Okinawa toward the end of the war in 1945, the island was frequently bombed by U.S. warplanes. The first thing that I found out upon arriving at the home island was that one of my aunts, that was my father's younger sister, had been killed by a U.S. Grumman fighter plane's strafing at our hamlet. It was a cold fact that the war killed my dear aunt, a simple, innocent woman on a remote tiny island, while I was away in mainland Japan.

After staying on the island for about two months, I planned to return to Kagoshima Normal School to complete the remaining year and a half of the six-year course. As there were no regular passenger boat services between the Amami Islands and mainland Japan, I asked for a ride aboard a ship which was pulling the Japanese army soldiers who had been stationed on Kikaijima to a port named Koniya on the larger island, Amami-Oshima, where the Japanese soldiers were gathered before they were returned to mainland Japan. There at Koniya, I found a clandestinely operated wooden boat, and I paid some amount of money to get a seat. There were about 50 people like me who were planning to go privately to mainland Japan. On our way to Kagoshima, our ship met with a storm and our ship had to put into a cove on Yakushima Island till the storm calmed down. Our boat safely arrived at Kagoshima Port. I returned to my school. Then, in the summer of 1946, I again wanted to go back to Kikaijima to spend the summer vacation, and I was able to get a ride aboard a ship carrying the repatriated Kikaijima-born soldiers who had served in different parts of Asia back to Kikaijima. After spending a month or so, I tried to return to mainland Japan to go back to my school. But at this time traveling between the Amami Islands and mainland Japan was very strictly controlled, because the Amami Islands and all the Ryukyu Islands had been cut off from Japan administratively. I went to the village office on Kikaijima to apply for a ticket to travel back to mainland Japan, but the village office people wouldn't even accept my application. If legal ways to go back to mainland Japan were not available, some other way should have been found out.

Many ships were transporting the Okinawan-born soldiers who had returned from war back to Okinawa. On their way back to Japan, some of these ships stopped by Kikaijima to procure brown sugar which was in great demand in mainland Japan right after World War II. My parents and I thought we should catch one of the ships which would stop by Kikaijima and ask for a ride. Then, one day, we saw a Japanese ship sailing toward Somachi Port on the northeastern part of our Kikaijima. We put some brown sugar in the bamboo basket and we hurried to Somachi Port to catch that ship. We knew a man at Somachi Port who had connections with those ships which stopped by Kikaijima to obtain precious brown sugar, which mainland Japan didn't produce. He took us to the ship and introduced us to the captain of the ship, telling him that I had to go back to school to graduate in March next. I told the captain that if I couldn't go back to school, the whole six-year education so far would be totally wasted. Then, the captain called his chief navigator and chief engineer, and asked for their opinions, telling them about my grave plight. I told them that I should go back to school by any means to graduate in March next year. They understood my situation and decided to give me a ride secretly to Kagoshima, where my school was.

I was very fortunate to get the ride aboard the repatriation ship. And I could go back to school, and I was able to graduate from Kagoshima Normal School in 1947. Then, I returned to Kikaijima and got a job teaching at a vocational high school there for one year. Then I took an examination to enter Okinawa Foreign Language School in September 1948, so that I might study English which I hadn't been able to study formally during the wartime. The Teachers' Room and classrooms were old Quonset huts and our dormitory a green tent camp on a hillside in the central part of Okinawa, which had been used by U.S. military forces during the battles of Okinawa. We students studied English as hard as we could. And the teaching method used by our school principal, Mr. Toshiro Onaga, was most impressive. He conducted his classes all in English, never using a word of Japanese! He showed us the importance of expressing ourselves in English by speaking. I admired his speaking ability and his fresh teaching method. I took a six-month teacher-training course there. I remember one of the teachers there taught us "Solitary Reaper" by William Wordsworth. Frankly speaking, my ability to understand and appreciate the English poem was not good enough at that time. And I also remember that I had immensely enjoyed reading old copies of *Reader's Digest* which U.S. servicemen had freely given away after reading them. On completing the six-month teacher-training course at Okinawa Foreign Language School in March 1949, I got a job at a motor pool in Kadena Air Base as an interpreter. One of my coworkers in the parts room was a Filipino named Hermenegildo Velasco, a very friendly Filipino. Then I moved to the Information and Education Section of the Ryukyu Military Government, which was located in Chinen in a southern part of Okinawa, and then the Military Government was moved to Naha, the central city of Okinawa. I was one of the translators. Our Section Chief was Ms. Evelyn Katsuyama, a University of Hawaii graduate, who was just as fluent in her Japanese as in her native English. She would look over our translations and edit them when necessary. All the experience I got there translating Japanese into English seems to have been very valuable to my later writing career. Then, there went an announcement in the newspapers that a group of young people would be selected and sent over to the United States for one year's study at an American college and that anyone interested should take the examination. It was a dreamlike opportunity for us young people in Okinawa and the Ryukyu Islands as a whole. So I took the examination and was lucky enough to get qualified to go over to the United States to study. A group of 52 young people from the Ryukyu Islands left Okinawa's White Beach aboard a U.S. military transport, U.S.N.S. *General Hugh Gaffey* on July 4, the Independence Day of 1950. That was the year when the Korean War broke out on June 25. Our ship stopped at Manila, Guam, and Pearl Harbor on our way to San Francisco. We arrived in San Francisco on July 26. The immensity of the San Francisco

Bay Bridge, spanning the great bay, was simply impressive. We took an orientation course at Mills College in Oakland for about five weeks. It was during our stay at Mills College that we got to see television sets at electric appliance stores in downtown Oakland for the first time in our lives. Upon finishing the orientation course, we were sent to different colleges and universities. Some of the people in our group of 52 of the year 1950 continued their studies and made significant achievements in their own fields, holding important positions toward the end of their careers. Their names and positions they held are: Toshio Akamine, professor at Washington State University; Yasuharu Agarie, president of Ryukyu University; Koji Taira, professor at the University of Illinois; Masanori Higa, taught at the University of Hawaii and Tsukuba University and was a professor at Ryukoku University in Kyoto; Mikio Higa, a vice-governor of Okinawa Prefecture. Some of them have already passed away, and I fondly think of them.

I was put in a group of 28 people who were sent to the University of New Mexico in Albuquerque, New Mexico. Mr. Edward Lueders and Miss Jane Kluckhohn were our English teachers there. That's how I got to know Edward Lueders and in time we got to form a lifelong friendship and started our literary collaboration. He and I launched on our project of translating some contemporary Japanese poetry into English in 1981 and after many years of collaboration, we finally got our translations published in a book, *Like Underground Water: The Poetry of Mid-Twentieth Century Japan*, (Copper Canyon Press, 1995), which is very popular.

At the University of New Mexico, I took such courses as anthropology, chemistry, European history, psychology, and physical education besides English reading and writing. What I learned in the chemistry course proved to be very valuable when I translated some anti-nuclear weapons poetry of Japan into English in 2007.

During the Christmas vacation of 1950, I visited the home of Mr. Kenkichi Masai, who had come over to America in 1914 and was running a flower business in Maspeth, Long Island. He was a man from a hamlet named "Aden" right next to my hamlet "Keraji" on Kikaijima. I had obtained his Long Island address from his parents on the island when I visited them before leaving for America. Mr. Masai's old parents, who were in their 80s at that time, told me to give their message to their son in America: "Come to see us while we are alive." I was very happy to tell Mr. Masai that I had seen his parents just before leaving the island for America. When I arrived at Mr. Masai's home in Maspeth, Long Island one December night in 1950, Mr. Masai and his American wife, Margaret, were very happy to see me, a boy from his home island. Right away, they took me to a restaurant in Chinatown of New York to celebrate my visit from Kikaijima. One day during my stay at his home, Mr. Masai asked me how long I would stay in America and I told him that I was studying in America under a one-year program and that I would be going back in June. Then he suggested that I stay in America until I complete a college education, offering to be my sponsor till I graduate from college in America. I had never expected such a great opportunity to come my way. Thanking him instantly for his generous offer, I immediately decided to extend my stay and continue my studies in America. After finishing my first year at the University of New Mexico, I came to Mr. Masai's home in Long Island and then I got a summer job as a dishwasher at a summer resort hotel, "Wentworth Hall" in Jackson, New Hampshire to make some money for my stay in America. I obtained my Social Security Account Card when I was working at Wentworth Hall, which I still have in my desk drawer as a memorable memento of my stay in America.

One evening during my employment at "Wentworth Hall," we had an "employees' picnic" by the lake near the hotel, and the American employees sang one song after another. Unfortunately, most of the songs were unfamiliar to me. And then, I was deeply touched by one particular song, the melody of which was so beautiful. The words of the song went like this: *"In the evening by the moonlight, you could hear those voices singing. In the evening by the moon light, you would hear those banjos ringing. How the old folks would enjoy it. They would sit all night and listen, as we sang in the evening by the moonlight…"* I still remember how deeply I was touched by that mysteriously beautiful song. But at that time I had never thought that I would get so much interested in American poetry in the future. After finishing my first year at UNM, I transferred to the New York State College for Teachers at Albany in the fall of 1951. Miss Vivian C. Hopkins was my English teacher and she greatly helped me get adjusted to the new environment in Albany. I would translate some old tanka of Japan into English and show them to Miss Hopkins. Then, one day she suggested that I write poetry instead of just translating tanka. Following her suggestion, I started to write something that looked like a poem. Then something very significant happened in the summer of 1953. After making up a few courses which I had failed in regular semesters in summer school, I got a job washing dishes at Saranac Inn in northern New York State. One night, after finishing the day's work, I took a walk by the lakeshore and I happened to see the most beautiful moon which I thought I had never seen before. The full moon looked so beautiful above the calm lake that I tried to write a poem, which turned out rather good. Returning to the fall semester, I showed it to Miss Hopkins, who suggested that I submit it to *The Christian Science Monitor,* which I did. *The Christian Science Monitor* accepted it. The poem is "Cave Man's Moonrise."(p.22)That was the happy beginning of my long career as a poet. Then, *The Christian Science Monitor* printed another poem of mine, "Unfolding Bud"(p.3) on July 13, 1957, and it has been reprinted in 8 school textbooks in America, Canada, Australia, and South Africa. Its most recent reprint is in *Literature: Steps to*

Success, (MacMillan Education, Australia, 2016). I have written hundreds and hundreds of poems good and bad in my life so far. And now I have selected about 200 poems of mine for this book. I have been grateful to all the editors and publishers who have printed my poems so far. I have been grateful to Stanley H. Barkan for printing some poems of mine both in English and Korean translation in his Korean Expatriate Literature anthology I and II. Since *Poetry Nippon* and *Mainichi Daily News* are no longer published, I have been submitting my poems to *POEMS OF THE WORLD* for nearly 20 years. The kind encouragement I get from Elma Photikarm, the editor of *POEMS OF THE WORLD* has been really inspiring, for which I have been very grateful. And I am grateful to all the foreign translators, such as Alessandro Dell' Anno, Paola Lucarini Poggi, Renzo Ricchi, Carmelo Mezzasalma, Zacharoula Gaitanaki, Yuhn-Bok Kim, Jung-Kee Lee, Myung-ok Yoon, Rachel S. Rhee, Kyung Hwa Rhee, Maxianne Berger, and others who have so kindly translated some of my poems into their languages.

By the way, I attended the 9th Mirbad Poetry Festival of the Arab World which was held in Baghdad from November 24 to December 1, 1988 and the entry in my diary on November 24, 1988 reads: "The 9th Mirbad Poetry Festival opened at the Conference Palace. The Minister of Information and Culture made an opening speech. Nizar Qalbani from Syria first read his poetry. Then, Abdul Wahid, the prominent Iraqi poet, read his poetry. Then, a poetess, from Kuwait, Su'ad Al-Subah, read her poetry. At night, I went to hear the poetry readings at Al-Rachid Theatre just across the street from Al-Mansour Melia Hotel. The readings by the poets of Arab countries were impressive, powerful, magnificent." On November 28, we had a bus tour to Babylon, and the old walls of the famous ancient city looked very impressive. We also visited the Museum of King Hammurabi. I still remember a bird which was singing very beautifully in the woods by the Museum. The entry in my diary on December 1 reads: "In the morning, a little before 10, we went to the Martyrs Monument. In the Hall at the base of the Monument about ten poets did their readings. The first reader was Mr. Wahid, the prominent Iraqi poet." One evening during my stay in Baghdad, I met a poet from Morocco at a coffee shop, and I wanted to know if my French could be understood by him, and I said to him, "I have a poem which I have written in French, entitled "A La Demoiselle." Would you please listen to me recite it, and see if you can understand my French pronunciation?" He said, "Go ahead. I'm glad to hear your poem in French." And I recited the short poem in French. The poem actually had been translated out of my English poem, "To a Young Lady."(p.126). Believe it or not, he said, "It's a good poem! I could understand your French!" It certainly was an interesting experience I had in Baghdad. How did I get to know French? I was taking a course in Shakespeare with Miss Vivian C. Hopkins in my 3rd year in college in 1953. When we came to Act III, Scene V of *Henry V*, I was shocked to find that the dialogue between Katherine, a princess of France, and Alice, an old French gentlewoman was being carried on in French, which I didn't know at all. I had never expected to come upon a dialogue in French in Shakespeare. So, I registered for a French course right in the next semester. I am glad I have studied French in my college days in America. I have translated three poems of mine into French. "To a Young Lady" is one of them.

By the way, I found a delightful poem, "Chaucer at the Game" by Robert Wallace in the October 2, 1959 edition of *The Christian Science Monitor.* The poem depicts the baseball game between the Red Socks and the Dodgers so interestingly in Chaucer's language that it just occurred to me that it would be fun to tinker with Middle English, imitating Chaucer. I have written quite a few poems in Middle English, and I have selected five and included them in SECTION 9. Eve Chambers, a friend of mine, and a couple of her friends liked my Chaucer poem, "Chaucer at the 50th Reunion" (p.210) so much so that I decided to include it in this book.

Now, I am grateful to John Dotson, the host of the *Ars Poetica* program of KAZU, Pacific Grove, Monterey Bay, Public Radio for reading and broadcasting 27 poems of mine with his guest, Deborah Keniston, on Valentine Day, February 16, 1988. I am very grateful to Stanley H. Barkan, Hassanal Abdullah, and Zhang Zhi, for their interest in my poetry. I warmly think of Patricia Holt and Carolyn Mary Kleefeld for their friendship, and I am also grateful to Marion Zoboski and Bruce Allen for their help when I translated many Japanese poems into English. I heartily thank Maxianne Berger for translating seven tankas of mine into French for the *Cirrus* magazine. I am also grateful to all the UPLI poets for their friendship and help. I'd like to thank all my friends whose names I can't mention individually. And I deeply thank Bruce Allen with all my heart for gracing this book with his kind INTRODUCTION.

And I also thank my Kikaijima friend, Eisuke Tomoda, for helping me with sending the manuscript to BookWay with his cyberskills. Finally, I thank Mr. Masafumi Kamigawa and other staff of BookWay for all the work they have so skillfully done in producing this book.

February 18, 2018

Naoshi Koriyama

SECTION 1

A LOAF OF POETRY

You mix
the dough
of experience
with
the yeast
of inspiration
and knead it well
with love
and pound it
with all your might
and then
leave it
until
it puffs out big
with its own inner force
and then
knead it again
and
shape it
into a round form
and bake it
in the oven
of your heart

BRING HIM A BRUSH

He tries to write a poem,
Every time something beautiful
Or something fresh
Touches his heart.
Now he looks at the mountain
Which is partly seen,
Through the white after-rain mist,
So exquisite and so serene.

After a hard search for words
And the way to put them together
In his endeavor
Of writing a poem of the scene,
He comes to realize
His poetic ability is not enough
To depict the mist-covered mountain.

Bring him a brush and a canvas!
Let him supplement his lacking words
With his brisk brush's strokes!

UNFOLDING BUD

One is amazed
By a water-lily bud
Unfolding
With each passing day,
Taking on a richer color
And new dimensions.

One is not amazed,
At first glance,
By a poem,
Which is as tight-closed
As a tiny bud.

Yet one is surprised
To see the poem
Gradually unfolding,
Revealing its rich inner self,
As one reads it
Again
And over again.

TO A POET

Fog, alone, cannot stand
Sunshine, time, or wind.
Fog is to fade away,
Erased by sunshine,
Absorbed by time,
Or carried away by wind.

Dear poet,
Scoop up the fog-like feeling, then,
With your aspiring hands,
And roll it up
Into a round, solid poem
Which can stand
Sunshine, time, or wind.

LIKE A MILKMAID

Like a milkmaid
squeezing milk
out of the udder
of her cow,

the poet squeezes
drops of poetry
out of his heart
in his lonely room.

AN AUTUMN SONG

A ball hit by a star player
cracks and soars
up the blue autumn sky,
as tens of thousands of fans roar
and whistle in excitement.

A poem I write
does not crack nor soar
in the blue autumn sky,
but only clicks
on my typewriter.

The ball hit by the star player
shines bright
in the front page article
of the sports papers
the following day.

Will the poem I have just written
ever have a chance
to leave my desk drawer
and soar up high in the hearts
of any future generation?

A TRANSLATOR'S MORNING RITUAL

Early in the morning
he reverentially sits
at his desk.
And he sharpens his pencils,
like a tiger sharpening his claws
in preparation for tearing apart a wild boar.

The tiger sharpens his claws,
scratching the hard trunk of a tree
in the dead silence
of the forest dense
with all his might,
with all his heart.

The translator sharpens his pencils
in preparation
for tearing apart some other poet's poems
to fill their skin
with the most delicious stuffing of his own cooking.

A NAMELESS PROFESSOR MAKES UP HIS MIND

At the bottom of the reverse side
of the final examination paper,
some of his students scribble:
"Dear Sir, I liked your poetry,"
"Your poetry was delightful,"
"Please keep on writing
more and more of your fine poetry."
Looking at the comments like these,
the nameless poet-professor
of a nameless university makes up his mind
to write something really good
that may someday make his students feel proud
of their nameless professor.

POET AS A BAKER

Your deep anguish, poet,
Is the dough
That makes your loaf of poetry.

Your irresistible urge, poet,
Kneads the dough
With all its might.

Your burning heart, poet,
Is the oven baking your anguish
Into sweet-smelling poetry.

AT THIS TIME IN HISTORY

At this time in history
when explosions and shootings are taking place in Iraq,
I look at the hibiscus flower
which has just opened
by the doorway of my home.
In this age of conflicts and violence,
artists should strive
to sing the beauty of nature,
the immensities of galaxies,
the boundlessness of the universe.
Let the Canadian dancers dance
with the aurora borealis dancing gracefully
in the northern skies.
Let the American poets sing
of the timeless grandeur of the Grand Canyon.
Let the archeologists of Wyoming dig up
the largest thigh bones of the dinosaur.
Let them contemplate the time
when the 100-foot seismosaurs roamed the prairies.
Let them think of man's unquenchable greed for power and wealth.
Let the poets of India sing of the towering Himalayas,
and I will stand by the doorway
of my humble home, looking at the hibiscus flower.
All the artists,
all the poets,
all the musicians
must sing of the grandeur
of the universe.
Let the world leaders think of the futility of their war

TO AN INACTIVE, SILENT POET

Why do you remain inactive,
silent,
mute,
voiceless,
these days?

Why don't you get mad
about the terrible disasters
at the Fukushima No. 1 nuclear plant?

Why don't you loudly cry,
looking at the cattleman's wife seeing her cows off hauled away
for disposal due to radioactive contamination?

Why don't you get angry
at your government trying
to export nuclear plants
to other countries,
when your own country is badly damaged
by the evils of the nuclear industry?

Man has been stealing energy
from the nucleus of the uranium atom
by splitting it arrogantly,
willfully,
in God's territory.
God will never allow man to infringe on His territory.

MY FINGERS BEGIN TO DANCE

It's a beautiful morning.
My wife finished washing clothes
and hanged them on the lines to dry
and is gone
to our neighbor's
for a friendly chat.
Here am I at my desk,
trying to squeeze some poetry
out of my heart
after a long lapse of languishing months.
It's good
to be writing something,
for a poet is a poet when he is writing something,
whether it's an immortal masterpiece or hopeless trash.
When I think I would write a classic that would remain
in world literature,
I would surely have a cramp on my shoulders.
When I think I would just write some simple, silly thing
that no one would ever remember,
my fingers begin to dance
on the keyboard of my word processor.

TRIBUTE TO THE USED RIBBON

This reel of ribbon,
Now dry and stained,
Has served me well,
Conspiring with me
To make hundreds of poems,
Lifting my heart
In the dark of night,
Eternalizing my dreams
In the light of day.

Working at my command,
Patient and quick,
This reel of ribbon
Has made solid and beautiful
What I found and brought
From the hills and stars.

WHITMAN BRISKLY STRODE

Did I briskly stride on the hill
of my home island
under the summer sun?
Did I stamp my feet hard
on the top of the hill
feeling some indescribable hunger
in my soul?
Did I howl to the stars
above the ceaseless sound
of the heaving sea?
Did I hit the ocean water hard
as I swam
along the rocky coral shore?

Whitman briskly strode
In the woods of Long Island
where white dogwoods blossomed
purple lilacs bloomed
and he howled
many a magnificent song
in his big resounding voice
deep in the pinewoods
of Huntington, Long Island
with his hands
reaching out
for the stars.

WHITMAN'S BROADWAY

He walked,
Whitman walked
along Broadway
in the warm afternoon sun
of 1850.
The buildings,
even the tallest buildings
along the street
were only five story high.
There were no subways, no buses,
no taxies.
Hatted gentlemen
and their long-dressed ladies
rode on two-horse wagons
and some men rode
on their horses
and a black dog
walked across the street
to the other side
where some tall yew-trees swayed
in the winds of May.

DID HE SEE?

In the long thinning streaks
of dark smoke
left by the Brooklyn ferry,
did Whitman see
in his mind's eye
a grand frame of steel beams
spanning the blue East River
from Manhattan
to Brooklyn?

In the white clusters
of stars above Manhattan
watching from his Long Island side,
did Whitman see
in his soul's eye
magnificent skylines
of towering skyscrapers
holding bright lights
among the stars?

UNDER YOUR KIND, FRIENDLY EYES
For Prof. Edward Lueders

Under your kind, friendly eyes,
my water lily bud opened
in the fresh morning air.
Under your interested eyes,
my jetliner took off
with its powerful engines fully open,
roaring loud,
soaring up and up
up into the chandelier of stars.

Prodded by your silent encouragement,
I kept making,
I kept making something,
I kept making something good,
I kept making something good enough
to meet your expectation.

Should my water lily ever remain in bloom
for many years to come,
and should my jetliner keep flying
all over the world
for many years to come,
it's all because I have made them good
just to live up to your expectation.

TO P. M.

On reading a commentary by P.M. on Hopkins' "Spring"

Much have I heard Lafcadio Hearn speak
   on "Manfred," "Grecian Urn,"
   on the beauty
   of the morning scene from the Bridge
   or on the singing Skylark pouring his heart.

Long have I stood beneath a persimmon tree,
   admiring the round, red, honey-packed fruits,
   thinking of my forty years that will not come again.

But never did I feel such keen joy,
   till I looked, following your direction,
   into the thrush's nest in the hedgerow,
   and saw heavens there in the blue, tiny eggs;
   till I heard the bird sing from the peartree top,
   rinsing and wringing my unaccustomed ears.

(An illustration taken from *Poems of the World*)

TO AN ENGLISH TEACHER IN JAPAN

On reading a commentary by Father Milward on Hopkins' "Spring"

Nothing is so delightful as this—
   when my groping eyes begin to see
   stars spangled on the thrush's blue, tiny eggs
   at the tip of your finger pointing at the nest;
   when my ears, having not heard any English thrush,
   begin to hear the clean, piercing song,
   looking at the bird sitting high on the peartree top;
   when I feel the blue descending from heaven
   down to the earth where little lambs romp.

What is all this wisdom and all this insight?
   I have seen Lafcadio Hearn set singing a nightingale
   from behind the beechen green for his students;
   I have also seen Blunden leading his disciples
   through a Wandering Wood, and past Error's Den;
   but did I never see heavens in thrush's tiny eggs:
   till you pointed at its nest in the hedgerow.

A GREAT TEACHER OF ENGLISH LITERATURE
Written for Father Milward's Book Launching

I stand by you,
watching Hopkins' windhover,
enthralled by its smooth, brave, graceful flight,
riding on and on, on the ever-rising air currents.

By the magic power of your commentary
the windhover of your country
will keep riding on the cool morning air
in the minds
of your students and friends
in our land of the Far East.

I can also hear the great gray drayhorse
making a loud battering sound
with the iron shoes that Felix Randal forged.

And now I stand by the hedgerow with you
and look
where your finger points
and there I see the thrush's tiny eggs
in its nest, shining bright,

and I dream
that the eggs
in the thrush's nest will hatch someday
and grow
and grow into full-fledged birds
and fly all over the hills and mountains,
filling the whole world
with their songs.

JANE TRINKLE READS MY POETRY ALOUD

My poetry,
a dull wingless hare,
is lifted
up
by the powerful wings
of a gigantic eagle
and
soars
up
and
up
riding
on ever-rising air currents
dancing
gliding
and turning
round and round
high up
in the open space
of the limitless sky

POETRY CLASS IN JAPAN

The teacher of English
Brings his students
All the way
Over several thousand miles
To Stoke Poges Church
And lets them sit and listen
To the poet Thomas Gray.

The teacher of English
Brings the poet Thomas Gray
All the way
Over two hundred years
Into the English class
And lets him speak
Of the pastoral life.

ADVICE TO A POET

Don't eat too much
of what you want to eat.
Beware of satisfaction.
Keep your stomach
always half filled,
for hunger alone will
make you aspire
to reach out for a star.

Don't you read too much.
Beware of others' words
filling up your heart.
Feel the warmth
of a baby's head
with your cheek
and think deep
on the fire of life
alone
and write
by a kerosene stove.

SECTION 2

CAVE MAN'S MOONRISE

Ever since man started to walk on the earth,
You have moved him with your beauty.
Speechless, he gazed upon you
From the mouth of his hillside cave.

The first word, I am sure, that he learned
   on the earth
Must have been a crude voice in praise of you.

Ever since his first words were learned,
He has sung myriad poems admiring you.

Therefore, I will not write a poem of you.
I shall just watch you tonight,
Sitting by the hushed shore of Saranac Lake,
Across the tranquil water of Saranac Lake.

THE AUGUST MOON

By the lunar calendar,
it's August 15 tonight,
the night we have the August full moon.
The moon the dinosaurs watched
in Wyoming's mountainsides
some 160 million years ago,
long before human beings came into being.
The moon Julius Caesar watched
in Rome 2,050 years ago.
The moon that has been shining on the Pyramids
for about 4,800 years, ever since they were built.
The moon the astronauts watched
through the spaceship's windows.
The moon that watched the debris of the bombed out cities
in the Second World War.
The moon under whose silvery beams countless men and women embraced.
The moon that has captivated human beings' hearts
ever since they started to walk on Earth.
Now
on the night of the August full moon,
I keep gazing on the moon
at a corner of a country in the Far East
in the evening of September 21, 2002.
This is one of the most precious moments
in my life.
So, I record this moment
in the annals of my life.

THE MID-AUTUMN FULL MOON

Today is August 15
by the lunar calendar,
so we have the mid-autumn full moon.

Many poets in ancient China and Japan
have written their poems
in praise of the mid-autumn full moon
since time immemorial.

And tonight
I look up at the most beautiful full moon
in my life
as intensely
as Su Shi of the Song dynasty of China did.

So many poets have written
so many poems in praise of the mid-autumn full moon,
and I too try to write mine,
looking at the brightest full moon.

Many of my island forefathers sang songs,
looking at the full moon
by the island shores,
listening to the sound of the ocean waves,
and tonight
I try to sing another song of mine
in praise of the mid-autumn full moon
in the suburbs of Tokyo,
far from the island shores.

THE NEW MOON

As I walk around the park
toward the evening
of May 4, 2003,
I look up
and happen to see
a thin new moon.
The moon has been the closest friend
to man
ever since he first looked up at it, wondering,
by the banks of the Nile,
or the Euphrates, or the Tigris, or the Yangtze,
or the lakeshores of Baikal.
How did the dinosaur gaze on the moon,
sitting on its haunches at the ridge of the Grand Canyon?
How did the ancient wolf howl
at the moon,
standing at the foot of Mt. McKinley?
How did my ancestors sing their folk songs
by the island shores
or how did they make love in the moonlight?
When I think of animals and human beings
that had looked at it
in their ephemeral sojourns on Earth,
I can't help thinking
about the influence of the moon,
about the timelessness of the universe.
The war that destroyed countless lives in Iraq
since March 2003 seems horrendous,
and yet vain at the same time.

THE FULL MOON

In an evening walk
One finds
All of a sudden
A great fresh golden egg
That the Swan has just laid
In the hollow
Of the deep pinewood

LET THE ADVANCED ASTRONOMER LOOK

Let the advanced astronomer look
Through the Hubble Space Telescope
Into the farthest galaxies
Of the bottomless universe,
Which ordinary humans can't see.
Let him examine the mysteries
Of the mysterious universe.

I'll stand by the roadside
At the foot of a *keyaki* tree
And keep looking at the moon,
Which countless human beings have watched
Ever since the beginning of time.
I'll keep admiring the beauty
Of the beautiful moon.

DISCOVERY OF A NEW PLANET

According to a newspaper article
of December 7, 2011
a new planet named Kepler22b
about 2.4 times the size of Earth
has been found
in what is called the "Goldilocks zone."
The article goes on to say, "The planet is 600 light years away.
It would take a space shuttle about 22 million years
to get there."
It is mind-boggling indeed
to me
who haven't been to Athens or Moscow
not to mention Greenland or the Antarctica.
I haven't seen the aurora borealis
in my life.
The most memorable place I visited
is the Great Wall of China.
I enjoyed watching the Constellation Swan,
standing by the shore
of my home island in summer.
Of course I can't see Kepler22b
with my naked eyes.
I just imagine myself riding on a space shuttle
darting through space
on a 22 million year mission
in my simple mind.

LOOKING AT VENUS

I walk my dog
around a wooded park
toward evening
all the year round,
witnessing the whole cycle
of the seasons' procession
in the budding,
      greening,
      yellowing,
      reddening,
      falling,
      and re-budding,
of the leaves of maples,
           dogwood,
           gingkoes,
           cherry trees,
in harmony with the eternal rhythm
         of the Earth
and from time to time
I raise my eyes
to look
at the Earth's companion planet, Venus,
shining bright
in the western sky.

TIME AND SPACE

The ocean liner
keeps on sailing
gallantly
riding over
heaving surges
of the open sea
as time flows on
ceaselessly
through
the heartbeat
of the passenger
who is leaning
against the railing
of the topmost deck
looking up
into the sky
where
millions of stars
too
are sailing
through
time
and
space
silently

A CAPTAIN'S MONOLOGUE

My heart beats
in harmony
with the pulse of the powerful diesel engines
of my ship
deep in the engine room,

while I keep watching the bow
bravely pushing through the rolling surges
in the summer sun
straight
on the course I have set,

and then at night
my soul sails through infinite space
from one constellation
to another,

as my ship keeps sailing
on the boundless sea

TWO UNIVERSES

I stood on the island hill, looking up
to scan the whole range
of the infinite expanse of the universe,
astonished
by the bright blinking stars
in the darkness of night,
and I thought,
"This is the grandest array of stars
no planetarium can ever hope to reproduce,"
and I was struck
by the naked grandeur
of the infinite universe.

And now sitting in the reclining seat
of the department store's eighth floor planetarium,
I look up
at the dome with a diameter of 60 feet,
and a height of 40,
simulating the evening sky
of March 31, 1990.
As the accelerated time progresses
within the dome
from the late afternoon to midnight,
bright stars appear all over the dome
ever intensifying their brightness,
striking my sense of wonder
and I find myself murmuring in my heart,
"Those projected stars are just as impressive
as the ones I see
on the hilltop of my home island."

ETERNAL GRANDEUR

I stand by the island shore
and look up at the stars above
spread out blinking all over the skies.
Up from the southern horizon
to the zenith of heaven
I slowly raise my eyes
And then on down to the northern sky
I swing my silent eyes
to trace the vast stretch of the Milky Way.
Galaxy beyond distant galaxy,
the mysterious universe expands
infinitely,
totally spellbinding my poor brains
with its vast immensity.
As I keep standing,
wondering about the mystery
of the very beginning
of the beginnings
of stars, of life, of dinosaurs' bones,
of whales' tails.
I don't even hear the sound of the sea,
my mind entirely engrossed
by the sheer unintelligibility
of time and space
and I keep standing
by the island shore.

THE ROCK AT THE EDGE OF THE TALLEST HILL

The rock at the edge of the tallest hill
on the island is rugged,
gray,
solid,
withstanding hard hailstones,
          cold north winds,
          deafening thunderclaps.
It has looked down
on the village below,
watching festivals,
weddings,
funerals,
and quarrels, since time immemorial.

In summertime, thunder clouds close in
from the horizon,
and then they hit the rock
with the most violent thunderbolts.

The rock has watched the Swan above at night
for countless ages.
It has seen young men leave the island
for military service in wars.
It has seen some U.S. fighter planes swoop down
and strafe at the village below.

Human babies are born,
grow up,
mature,
some leaving the island,
others remaining on the island,
 living their individual lives,
while the rock on the hill remains still,
looking down on the village below.

ON HIS GRANDMA'S ISLAND

The city-bred boy stands
on the very top
of the tallest hill
on his grandma's island
that lies alone
in the world's largest sea,

and he looks
over the ocean's wide, wide horizon
from its one end…slowly…to the other

and suddenly notices
that the horizon far is slightly curved
against the blue background of infinite skies

and he is surprised
by the vast, magnificent curvature
of the world's largest sea

and says to his father,
"Oh, I think I can see
the earth is 'slightly' round."

THE RAGING SEA IN A TYPHOON

Unleashed from the moon's tether,
Set on wild by the shouting winds,
Mountainous waves now
Come charging,
Like maddened mastodons,
Clashing, dashing,
Roaring, and baring their fangs white
And jump
At the sharp-edged rocks
Of the island's coral shores,
Shaking the whole island to its root,
Then retreating some distance
Only to repeat the furious attack
With even still greater force and rage.

EARTH DAY 1990

Now we have come
from every corner of the world
to the Earth Day events
to celebrate
the beauty of our Planet Earth,
to denounce
the ugliness of human greed,
to celebrate
the joy of watching sunsets and stars,
to denounce
the foolishness
of war,
to celebrate
the splendor
of oceans and mountains,
to cry over
the danger
of destroying the rain forests,
of polluting the air and water and land.
We have come here
in search of ways
to save our ailing Earth.

REMINISCENCE

Standing alone
on the top
of the hill
on the small island
I would often look
east
and see the Pacific Ocean gently heave
as far as its horizon
and then
I would turn
all round west
to look and see
the East China Sea,

and now
far away from the island
I sing
in my heart
the sweet folk melody
that our forefathers
have picked
from the ceaseless beat
of the ocean waves
that keep breaking
on the coral shores.

SUMMER ON THE HOME ISLAND

The man stops his bicycle
on the hillside road

that runs through
the sugarcane fields

and he gets off the bicycle
and takes off his sandals

to feel the texture
of his home island's earth

to feel the warmth of the earth
heated by his home island's sun

with his bare unshod feet
with his free naked heart

looking over the hill
listening to the sound of the sea

HARVEST

When the earth was frozen,
The air cold,
The larks silent,
The farmers sowed
The seeds of wheat
With their hands stiff with cold
But their hearts full of hope.

When the earth is soft,
The air warm,
The larks loud,
The farmers reap
The golden grains
With their hands perspiring
But their hearts full of thanks.

A THOUGHT BY A MOUNTAIN STREAM

The coolness…
the special coolness
of this mountain stream
as I dip my feet
in the water
suddenly makes me think
of those rustic, robust forefathers
of ours
who must have squatted here
ages and ages ago
right on this stone
to scoop up the water
in the cup of their palms
or bathed in this stream
washing away their dirt and sweat
after long hard work
in the fields or woods or hills
on this small remote island
in the middle of the heaving sea

A VIEW OF EXPO '70 JUST BEFORE CLOSING
For James Kirkup

We are about to leave this new, man-made moon.
To leave this City of Fantasy
Is to take one last irretrievable step back into reality, the commonplace,
Into our daily lives. From moving walkways, from spiral steel stairways,
We look up at the bright Tree of Light and the gigantic Sky Hook of Australia.

We have seen close-up the Tree of Life, the Tower of the Sun.
Here spaceships both Russian-made and American-made lie at anchor.
We roam about this new world, flooded with the weird sound of electrons.
And in the mazes among strange structures we grown-ups too can get lost.

Standing by the dancing fountains, climbing up the Tower of the Sun,
We marvel at the grandeur of what the human spirit can create.
Yet, in the well-displayed rooms of pavilions, these fantastic structures,
We are struck more by the shining beauty of the young women of various lands

But let us always remember, beyond the wonders and beauties that we see,
Our fallen cosmonauts, our brave workmen who did not safely return
From their risky missions aboard iron beams high up in the sky,
Those heroes who dedicated their very lives to make possible these festivities.

KINKAKUJI TEMPLE
Kyoto, Japan

The six-hundred-year-old pond
calmly sustains
the dream-like image
of the Golden Temple.

Only occasionally
a large carp or two
break the smoothness
of the ancient pond,
peeping out of the shade
of the lotus pads.

No, even the carp are aware
of the weight of time,
and careful
not to break
the timeless image
of the Golden Temple.

BY THE LAKESHORE
Hokkaido, Japan

Long before the boathouse speakers
   chased the water rails and wild ducks
     from their quiet nests deep in the reeds,

long before the merry ferries broke
   the tranquility
     of this beautiful lake,

long before the rushing train's whistle
   shook off soft-piled snow
     from the trees on the lake islets,

Oh, did some Ainu lad pipe his reed from a canoe,
   calling his love across the lake?

Oh, did his sweetheart answer the call,
   gently swaying a willow's branch?

LAKE OHNUMA

Where are the water fowls
that used to sit
in their nests
deep in the reeds?

Where are the squirrels
that used to climb the trees
picking nuts
in full delight?

Where are the Ainu lads
that rowed their canoes
across this tranquil lake
to serenade on the opposite shore?

Ay, where are the Ainu girls
that gently touched
fresh-opened water-lilies,
waiting for their boys' canoes?

AT THE WONDERFUL CALL

At the wonderful call
of a bush warbler
in the tree by the country road
I stop my bicycle and stand.

From out of the thick leaves
of the tree,
the bush warbler calls again.
I mimic his call
with my whistling.
Then, he calls again
in response
to my mimic warbling.
We exchange our friendly playful calls
with each other.
As I look into the tree,
he is busily moving from one branch
to another,
responding to my call.
His singing is not so skillful yet in April,
but very friendly.
We enjoy exchanging our calls
for some time
in the spring afternoon sun.

A BUSH WARBLER CALLED

It was around seven in the morning
on March 20, 2001
that I heard a bush warbler call
from the pine tree in our yard.
I couldn't quite believe my ears,
for we seldom see any bush warbler around
in our urban neighborhood.
My wife called,
"Look, he's in the pine tree."
We listened
and listened to his song.
Then, he was gone,
gone like the Nightingale in *Rubaiyat* of Omar Khayyam:
"The Nightingale that in the branches sang,
Ah, whence, and whither flown again, who knows!"
I don't know in what deep woods he was hatched
out of a tiny, green egg,
nor do I know why he came to our yard to sing.
Of course, he couldn't have thought:
"There's a poet in this house
who hasn't written a line of poetry
ever since he wrote his New Year's Day poem.
So, I'll stop by his pine tree
and sing of the beauty of his plum blossoms
to wake him up,
and shake him,
and inspire him to start singing again like me."
And that was exactly what he did.
He woke me up.
He shook me from my long languidness.

ON THIS SPRING DAY

I walked to the post office.
I walked to the photo shop.
I walked to the bookstore.
I walked to the convenience store.
I did all this
just to walk under the overhanging cherry blossoms,
under the soft, pinkish clouds of cherry blossoms
in the daytime today.

And at night
the cherry blossoms in full bloom are lit up
by the streetlights.
As I look up,
I happen to see the bright Evening Star, through the break
of the pinkish clouds
of cherry blossoms,
the Evening Star that Sappho saw and sang
on her Greek island
some 2,600 years ago,
the Star that countless other poets too have sung
all over the world
throughout human history,
admiring its brightness.

TO THE SWAN

Are you on your way to a neighboring universe,
carrying God on your huge, graceful wings?

Or are you headed for a distant lake
on His eternal boundless estate?

Billions of eyes, awe-struck,
have watched you flying thus

ever since man first looked up at brand-new skies,
and we too watch you tonight…

Before long our eyes
will be closed forever,

but you will keep flying eternally
   freezing billions more souls
      into a helpless, dreaded silence…

LET THE FISH HAPPILY SWIM

Let the freshwater fish happily swim
in the lakes and rivers up in the mountains.
Let the hordes of whales cruise
all over the oceans
all year round.
Let the little playful white-saddled reef fish look
into my underwater goggles
as I watch him hover
over his coral tree.
Let the birds keep singing
in the woods
all over the Earth.
Let the gorillas survive
in the mountains of Africa.
Let the giant pandas mate
in their native habitats of China.
We human beings have no right
to pollute the waters and air and forests and seas
with filthy, toxic chemicals
and deadly radioactive materials.
And we have no right
to fight
a nuclear war.

(As illustrated in *Poems of the World*)

A GARDENER

I see two bamboo brooms
and a basket
at the entrance
to his garden.
Over many years
he has been the master
of this garden,
pulling weeds in the grass
on hot summer days,
sweeping fallen leaves
late in the fall,
shoveling snow
off the garden's paths
in winter,
while world politics revolved,
yens and dollars fluctuated,
stocks rocked restlessly,
business swayed up and down,
blood was shed
in crime-ridden cities
and in war-torn lands.

CHESTNUTS ARE FULL AND RIPE

Chestnuts are full and round and ripe.
They are
the wonderful outcome
of nature's mysterious work.

They shine
with a bright brown luster.

They grew and developed on the tree
every day,
rain or shine.
all summer.
Now
it's autumn,
the season of fullness,
the season of roundness,
the season of ripeness.

And we receive,
enjoy,
appreciate, value,
and thank,
all the wonderful result
of nature's work.

ON THE EVENING OF APRIL 6, 2001

On the evening of April 6, 2001
I was walking toward the public library
to read a newspaper article.
At the entrance
I happened to cast my eyes toward the west,
and saw the most glorious sunset
beyond pinkish clouds of cherry blossoms.
I had never seen such a majestic sunset
in all my life,
so big, so perfectly round,
reddish orange, embossed on the darkening sky.
I stood for a while,
struck by the beauty
of the center of our solar system,
the very source of all life,
past, present, and future.
But I wrenched myself
from the joy of admiring the beautiful sun
to read a mere newspaper article
written by a mere human being.
After reading it, I came out
only to find the glorious sunset gone.

Didn't I make a foolish mistake?

LOVELIEST OF TREES, THE CHERRY NOW

That English poet, A. E. Housman sang
"Loveliest of trees, the cherry now
Is hung with bloom along the bough…"

And now I stand by a cherry tree
In full bloom here in Japan,
Flaunting its pure beauty.

Let Housman sing his immortal poem
About his cherry tree of his England.
I will stand here by my cherry tree.

I will stand and keep looking up
At the magnificent blossoms.
Let me feel their beauty here and now.

So many poets have sung so many poems
In praise of cherry blossoms in the world.
Now let me try to add just one more.

SWEETEST-SCENTED OF BLOSSOMS
For A. E. Housman

Daphne blossoms begin to bloom
early in March here in Sagamihara,
emitting their most superb fragrance
all around.
Even in the complete darkness
of night
I can "see" where the scent comes from
and can "hear" spring announcing its arrival.
In our front yard
we have two daphne bushes.

Every time I pass,
I stop
and stand
and stoop
to bring my nose to the blossoms,
taking a deep, deep breath
over and over again,
hearing that English poet speaking to me
from behind:
"Of your lifetime
threescore years and thirteen will not come again.
To smell the daphne blossoms in bloom
what few years you have left are little room."
So I keep on smelling the sweetest scent
with all my heart.

MYSTERIOUS IS THE UNIVERSE

The book about the universe says:
"The universe got started
with the 'Big Bang'
and has expanded
to its present size
in 13.7 billion years,"
and
"It is certain
that the universe is still expanding."

And I'm puzzled by the information
and go out into my humble garden,
to look at the daffodils in bloom
in the cold winter sun,
at the beginning of February, 2011.

And the book goes on to mention,
"Nobody knows whether the universe will keep expanding
forever
or it will stop expanding
at a certain point
and then begin shrinking."

It certainly is mysterious
that I feel like writing poetry
looking at the daffodils in my garden
on the tiny planet
in the ever-expanding universe.

THE MOON IS BEAUTIFUL TONIGHT

The moon is beautiful tonight.
I look at it.
I gaze on it.
I peer at it.
I praise its beauty.
I admire its brightness.
I worship its perfect roundness.
I call on every single word I know
to describe the beauty of the moon.
I wonder how a lone wolf howled its first howl
at the ancient moon rising
above the mountain.
I wonder how ancient people wondered
at their ancient moon rising above the lake.
I wonder how future human beings will admire the moon
in countless generations
on the Earth,
peering at it
from the promenade deck
of some super-modern cruise ship,
from their stupendously tall skyscrapers,
or through their newest telescope.

TO THE PERSIMMON TREE

Shake off
The dry, faded leaves
With the cool winds.

Deepen the red color
Of your fruits
By putting them
Against the blue winter sky.

Make rounder still
Your round fruits
With sweet juice.

Change them
Into lumps of honey
With the cold frost.

THE EARTH RIPENS

The earth ripens
and persimmons mellow.
After mellowing as much as they can
they fall.
On the ground in the autumn air
the sugar inside the bright golden fruit
begins to ferment,
turning into elixir.
Then the harvest mouse comes out
to sip the wine
and begins to dance
under the harvest moon.

ON THIS FINE AUTUMN MORNING

On this fine autumn morning
I find a hibiscus flower
in bloom
at the doorway,
and greet it
with all my love.

On this fine autumn morning
I pick up a most beautiful persimmon leaf
at the foot
of our persimmon tree,
holding it
in my hand
most reverentially.

On this fine autumn morning
I look up
at the ripening persimmons,
admiring their roundness,
praising their brightness,
thinking of their mellow sweetness
with all my heart.

THE PERSIMMON TREE

The persimmon tree in our yard
on its branches has rich reward
for its tireless, diligent work.
Dark and rough is the tree's bark.
Under it the earth's nutriment
keeps going up for the enrichment
of each round growing persimmon.
Water, earth, sunlight in unison
work together to make the fruit grow
round, big, bright, and mellow.
Autumn is the time of fruitfulness.
Looking at the tree's richness,
I find myself in my life's autumn.
I rush this poem, hearing the drum
of Time that tells me of the end
of my life I am to comprehend.

I GO OUT INTO THE YARD

I go out into the yard
in the morning sun.
The autumn air is cool.
I stand under the persimmon tree,
its branches heavy with fruits,
solid, full, cool and bright.
I touch one persimmon
after another
in admiration,
the result of nature's long, steady work
ever since its very first inception in buds,
through white blossoms, tiny lumps,
and ceaseless growth in spring,
in the scorching summer sun
and the mild autumn sun.
And now the persimmon is
as solid as its steady process,
as full as its ceaseless growth,
as cool as the autumn air,
as bright as a ripe persimmon can be.

WINDLESS WOOD

Over the white soft sand
The thin green needles
Of the seaside pines
Are still and songless
Like the painted pine
In an Oriental scroll.

Through the brown hard trunks
And the deep green needles
Thin spring rain falls silent
Upon the white soft sand.
Some of the pine leaves point upward;
Some down.
Look up there.
On the tip of each down-pointing needle
A tiny glittering pearl is formed
By the thin spring rain
In this windless seaside wood.

ESSENCE OF MORNING

At the sharp-pointed tip
Of the snake-gourd's polygonal leaf,
A large dewdrop,
Fresh and shining,
Sustains itself,
Crystallizing
At that ephemeral but absolute point
All the freshness
And all the coolness
Of this clear autumn morning.

"Essence of Morning" drawn by the author

THROUGH THE WINDOW

Through the window
I see the soft rain.

Through the soft rain
I see the neighbor's fence.

And just above the fence
I see fully opened umbrellas
Softly flowing from left to right
On and on.

Hidden by the neighbor's fence
I cannot see
Who goes there
Under each of the umbrellas.

But, I see each umbrella
Softly flowing from left to right
On and on,
Shading the someone under it
In the soft morning rain.

LET ME SEE YOUR BEAUTY

Let me see your beauty,
you, daffodils.

Let me smell
your sweet fragrance.

Thank you for blooming
in our garden,

in this noisy, violent, difficult world
of the 21st century,

brightening all the air
of our garden.

Let your beauty brighten
the entire world now.

Let your fragrance fill
the entire world now.

WALK SLOWLY

Walk slowly,
Ever slowly
Along the avenue
Of cherry trees in full bloom.

Don't even talk.
Don't ride a bicycle.
Just walk slowly
Under the clouds of cherry blossoms.

Hold these holy moments
In your hands.
Just grab these delightful moments
In your hands.
Cherish these precious moments
In your heart.

For tomorrow
The petals may begin
To fall
From the cherry blossoms.
So, savor the delicious moments
In your heart,
As you walk along the avenue
Of cherry trees in full bloom.

SEA TURTLE HATCHLINGS

Overflowing with vital energy,
The sea turtle hatchlings crawl
Out of the sand
Into the world,
Madly scrambling
To get into the sea.

Directed by instincts,
They know
Where to go.
They madly crawl
In the direction
Of the sea.

On the white sand,
They make their way
Toward the sea,
Scratching the sand,
Leaving the marks
Of their first struggle on Earth.

(As illustrated in *Poems of the World*)

SO INNOCENT, SO BUSY

Warmed by the heat
of the sun,
eggs of sea turtles develop
into beating hearts,
into hatchlings,
in the sand
by the sea,
and now out they crawl
from the sand
into the world
under the sun.

So innocent, so busy,
they madly crawl
toward the sea,
taking their first breaths
under the sun.
Completely unaware of the wars
and conflicts
in the human world,
they busily crawl to the sea.

They are the heartbeats
of the Supreme Being
in the mysterious universe.
They are the breaths
of the Supreme Being
in the mysterious universe.
They are the fingertips
of the Supreme Being
in the mysterious universe.

TWO PENGUIN CHICKS

Two penguin chicks romp
around their mother
on the TV screen showing some island
in the Antarctic.
They just can't keep still.
Energy emanates
from their young bodies.
The joy of being alive explodes
out of their young hearts.
Their mother seems
to be telling them to be quiet,
but they just can't stay still
under the sun that's new to them
upon the earth that's new under their feet.

THE GENTLE-EYED HIGHLAND BULL

His horns are long,
Sharp,
Formidable,
Making some tourists feel a little afraid.

They could break anything soft and daft
With a single blow.

They could whistle shrilly
Over the heaths
On the Highlands
In the north wind.

But his eyes are so gentle,
Innocent,
Looking at the interested tourists.
His hair too is long,
Partly covering his gentle eyes.

Then, he softly moos
With a Gaelic accent.

THE SUNSET

Nothing is as glorious as the sunset.
The large, round, golden sun is going down
In the west, over the mountain.
I stand here still
To adore its glory.
I stand here still
To sing the happiest song
In my life.
I stand here still
To feel the greatest joy
In my life.
I stand here still
To paint the most beautiful picture
In my life.
I stand here still
To witness the most brilliant brushwork
Of the Greatest Artist.

AN IMAGE OF A HORSE

The bright morning sun leaps out of the ocean
and the horse on the island awakens,
and yawning a big, sleepy yawn,
he draws the cool, clean, fresh air
deep into his lungs
and then he rears, with his proud head high
against the blue, clear sky,
projecting a huge shadow
on the screen of the steep upright cliff
and then he kicks on the grass
and jumps,
and begins to gallop.
His pent-up energy explodes,
kicking up a cloud of dust, dust of coral sand,
as high as the island's tallest hill,
his hoofs trampling hard on the hard rocky road,
and the sound of the hoofs hits the side of the hill
and its echo sails over the waves of the sea
as far as the vast curved horizon.
The puffs of breath out of his angry nostrils form
bright, big rainbows in the sky.
The bulging lumps of muscles on his back
shine bright, touched by the morning sun.
Galloping wild to his fill,
he now comes to a stop,
and his sudden neigh shakes the eggs in the owl's nest
atop the pine on the crest of the hill.

KIKAI ISLAND OF AMAMI IN SOUTHERN JAPAN

There is one of the smallest islands there
on the western edge of the largest ocean.
It faces the Pacific on the east.
It faces the East China Sea on the west.
Those on eastern shores have greeted the sun
rising out of the wide, wide horizon.
Those on western shores have fondly admired
the most beautiful sunsets all year round.
Children returning from school often see
dolphins roll and jump on the surging surface
of the ever-flowing Japan Current.
The tallest hill is 700 feet high.
From the soaring crest of Mt. Everest
you can't see the roundness of our great Earth,
but from the tallest hill of the island,
you can see the Pacific horizon
showing the grand curvature of the Earth,
extending from the south far to the north.
When you stand by the shore at summer night,
looking up into the sky above your head,
you can see the magnificent, grand Swan
eternally flapping its widespread wings
through vast space of the boundless universe.
You can almost hear the Swan's wings whistling
above the sound of restless ocean waves
ceaselessly breaking against coral shores.
But World War II cast its dark, sad shadow.
119 islanders were killed
in frequent air raids by U. S. warplanes.
Two U. S. pilots shot down were caught and killed.
Of course, they had their families back home.
Their wedding rings shone in the island sun.
Nothing is more precious than peace on Earth.

In the gentle moonlight by the seashore
island people sing their loveliest folk songs,
strumming snakeskin samisens by the sea.

A TOMB ON AN OKINAWAN HILL
A scene seen in 1948 and recollected in 1979

On a secluded slope
Of an Okinawan hill
Covered with pampas grass
Is a deserted tomb

A few years ago
Violent naval bombardments
Shook the whole island
And the brown bones
Of those village ancestors
Must have rattled
In the dark
      of the tomb

And now
As some students
Of the small English-language school
On the hill
Walk down the path
Toward the lighted village below
A lone firefly
Flickers its lantern
In the dew-wet grass
By the old deserted tomb

MAN AGAINST NATURE

The maddened power shovel
is sinking his sharp, silver teeth
deeper
and deeper
and deeper still
into the bleeding sides of the hill,
shaking his own entire body,
stamping and straining his flat iron feet,

not caring a whit
about the desperate call
of the finch that is claiming
her territory
from the tip of the tallest pine
atop the hill

A RAINBOW IN THE SKY

Although the rain now
is full of acid
and the air
polluted
with smoke
and various oxides,
of nitrogen,
of carbon,
of sulfur and what not,
nature has not quite forgotten
her art.
Lo!
She can still paint
a beautiful rainbow
on the canvas
of the murky late afternoon sky
with such superb strokes
of her brush!

OIL CRISIS

When our last drop
of oil
has been used up
and all our cars
come to a stop
and all our planes
begin to rust
on the runway
in the rain
and the lights
go out
from the soaring skyscrapers
we will walk
to the hill
to pick
raspberries wild
and steal
dappled eggs
from quails' nests
and then
we will walk
down to a stream
and catch eels
and by night
we will sit
by the river's bank
looking up
into the clear silent sky
reading poetry
in the stars

KINGLY MOUNTAIN
Mt. Sakurajima

Toy-like are the steamers on sea.
Cork-like are the breakwaters off the piers.
Box-like are the concrete buildings of town.

Looking down on all of these,
You sit grand,
As majestic as a king.
On the blue carpet of the calm bay
Your lofty throne is securely set,
With your pages of honor,
The mist-covered low mountains, following
To your sides right and left.

Yellow volcanic sand crowns your top;
The May-bright green of the trees
And the brownish gray of the rocks
Dress your massive sides.
Your stately figure
Presides firm and great
Over the bay and the city.

"Kingly Mountain" drawn by the author

MT. SAKURAJIMA PUTS ON A SHOW

"An inestimably long time ago
A tiny piece of fire
Had been shaken off
From the spinning, flaming sun.
The little piece of fire,
Left alone in the frigid, dark, abysmal sky,
Has lost some of its heat,
And has come to be our solid Earth."

This is what I have heard
About the origin of this planet.

The Earth, however, has cooled off—
Not to a large extent yet.
Beneath its seemingly firm eggshell
Melted rock is still boiling.

Come, astronomers and earth scientists.
Come to this city of Kagoshima, Japan,
To watch the restless volcano
Which has just knocked its crater open wide,
Puffing up a heroic, bulging column of smoke
Six thousand feet into the clear autumn blue.

THE BRIGHTEST MOON ABOVE MT. SAKURAJIMA

The brightest,
freshest,
fullest moon
just as bright and fresh
as it was
when
it once shone
into sleeping dinosaurs' closed eyes
on the great prairies
of Planet Earth
now
hangs
just above
the dark, clam figure
of Mt. Sakurajima
and its shadow
broken
into millions of golden pieces
dances
and leaps
on the rippling surface
of Kinko Bay.

LOOKING UP AT MT. FUJI

Twelve hundred years go
Our ancient poet praised
In his simple and forceful words
Your grandeur, your magnificence,
Looking up at you
From his humble thatched hut,
From the green shrubby hill,
Or his floating skiff on the bay.

And in recent years
Countless poets and non-poets alike
From many other lands
Have come here
Jut to admire you.

Beautiful you are,
When an evening sun casts its pinkish rays
Over the snow on your top;
Grand,
When the blue autumn sky
Makes loftier your lofty stance;
Majestic,
When a white cloud softly wafts
By your noble shoulders in summer.

On these low shrubby hills
The azaleas are blooming,
White, pink, purple, and red,
In the bright spring sun,
While the warblers are joyously calling
From the shade of the new-green shrubs.

Here I stand on the green hill,
Looking at your soaring throne
 In joy, in praise, and in rapture

BEHOLDING MT. FUJI

No word can fully express
How uplifted I feel,
As I stand here,
Gazing upon the soaring Peak
Of Mt. Fuji.

Entranced I stand,
Feeling again the long-forgotten comradeship
That has existed
Between Man and Nature
Ever since the beginning
Of Man's life on this Earth.

Modern man, who is too busy
To pause and praise
The blooming azaleas
At his own doorway plot,
Should come here
Just once in a while
To watch the heart-lifting high mountain,
Sitting by the hillside trail,
Listening to the bush warblers' calls
In the clear mountain air.

Oh, mountain magnificent!
You are ever a friend to Man,
Ever telling us to lift our eyes
To your grand soaring height.

THE EAGLE IN CAPTIVITY

Your powerful wings once whipped the cool mountain air,
whistling loud in the limitless sky.
Your eyes would stare,
from the height of your mountaintop,
at any moving object far down below.
You have watched many glorious sunsets
from the edge of the loftiest cliff.
Your claws have often crushed the ribs
of a screaming monkey
on the windy crag
of a steep mountainside.
Your sharp beak has often broken the neck
of a helpless hare
with a single blow.
Now you perch
on the man-made mock tree branch
within the zoo's iron bars.
On the wet concrete floor
I see eight chicken heads scattered about,
which your sense of pride wouldn't let you touch.
Dulled by the confinement,
your eyes have now lost their fierce glare.
We no longer hear your beautiful cry.
Now you blandly look
into the windows
of the art museum
right next to your cage.
Your powerful wings will no longer whip the air
in the blue of the open sky.

THE EAGLE IN THE CAGE

From the concrete platform
in the cage
of the zoo
the golden eagle slowly lifts himself,
flapping his wide wings,
fanning the warm, stagnant air
of the narrow space
and flies
in a circle
round and round
for three times,
dreaming that he is soaring
up a precipitous mountainside
under a blue open sky
looking down
on a magnificent river flowing on
far toward the horizon.

HYMN TO THE GRAND CANYON

What did the dinosaurs think with their brains
as they looked at the immense expanse
of the lofty, steep mountainsides
some 65 million years ago,
when there were no human beings on the planet?
For ages and ages,
long before man invented the flying machine,
only hawks and eagles cast their shadows
over the stupendous, overwhelming cliffs,
riding on the rising air currents
blowing upward from the bottom of the deep gorge below.
Long before the Indians came,
only coyotes howled their hymns
to the Grand Canyon
deep at night,
looking over the moonlit grandeur.
The first Indians walked a long distance
of time and space
from the land of their ancestors in Asia.
Ever since Garcia Lopez de Cardenas looked
at the immensities,
awe-struck,
in 1540,
millions and millions of people made pilgrimages
to these enormous sculptures carved by the Creator.
And now my wife and I have come
to this Greatest Wonder of the World,
uttering our fascination
in our own language.
Layer over layer of ruddy rocks reveal
the prodigious power of God's sharp, tough chisel,
taking away our humble breaths.
I slowly scan the vastness of the Grand Canyon
from south to north, from west to east,

trying to feel the space of time
that the Greatest Wonder has stood
in eternity.
My soul feels infinite veneration
for this majestic masterpiece of the Creator,
but how can I ever depict its grandeur
in words?
Giving up my attempt at describing its magnitude,
I look up
and see the clear, blue, silent sky.

GRAND CANYON IN THE SUN

Even God Almighty has taken
millions and millions of years
to carve out
those immense, holy, ruddy sculptures soaring
up into the blue skies,
His sharp chisel cutting deep
to the bones
of Planet Earth
since time immemorial.

Let the minds of human beings reflect
on the vanity
of fighting
over petty differences
in religions, politics, economic systems.
Let the hearts of human beings sing
of the grandeur
of the Grand Canyon glowing
in the sun.

LOOKING OVER THE GRAND CANYON

Peoples come from all over the world and praise the Grand Canyon in their own languages.
Australians acclaim, "Awe-inspiring!" with their Australian accent.
Belgians bet, "Breath-taking is the Grand Canyon!"
Chinese chant, "Charmingly majestic!" in Chinese.
Danish tourists declare, "Dazzling! Devastating!" in Danish.
Egyptians exclaim, "Enormous! More enormous than our Pyramids!"
French folk flatly swear in French, *"Fantastique!" "Formidable!"*
Greeks gasp, "Great! Gorgeous! Grandiose!" in Greek.
Hungarians howl, "Holy smoke! Horrifying!" in Hungarian.
Indians interject, "Indescribable! Incredible!" in Hindi.
Japanese judge, "Jumbo! Just magnificent!" in Japanese.
Koreans call, "Colossal! Crushing!" in Korean.
Lithuanians lisp, "Lofty! Lordly!" in Lithuanian.
Mongolians muse, "Majestic! Marvelous!" in Mongolian.
Norwegians note, "No comparison!" in Norwegian.
Okinawans orate, "Overwhelming! Outstanding!" in their island language.
Peruvians proclaim, "Petrifying! Prodigious!" in Spanish.
Qataris quip, "Quite fantastic!" in their own language.
Romanians repeat, "Remarkable! Remarkable!" in Romanian.
Swiss scream, "Stupendous! Startling!" in French, or German, or Italian.
Tunisians twitter, *"Trop grande! Trop grande!"* in French.
Ukrainians eulogize, "Utterly unearthly!" in Ukrainian.
Venezuelans voice, "Very impressive!" in Spanish.
West Indians warble, "Wonderful, indeed!" in their island language.
Xhosas exclaim, "Extraordinary!" in their South African language.
Yugoslavians yell, "You can't beat it!" in the Yugoslavian language.
Zairians zealously shriek, "Zonking is the Grand Canyon!"
But no language on Earth can sufficiently describe the real grandeur of the Grand Canyon!

SECTION 4

AT A GARDEN IN KYOTO

Looking at Mr. and Mrs. Edward Lueders

Don't talk to them.
Just let them sit—
Sit there speechless
As long as they please
On the stone bench
By the edge
Of the pond
Where water lilies bloom
And carp swim.

Don't you talk to them.
Just let them feel
The peace
Of this pond
To their fill.

Let them dream
Of the shrewd mind
Of the ancient landscape architect
Who could scoop up
And steal the beauty of nature
With his hoe.

PROFESSOR PERRY D. WESTBROOK

I was not a bright student,
but bright enough
to sense that you were a great teacher.
You were not a flamboyant lecturer.
You spoke rather quietly,
but I could see
that your statements were incisive,
as incisive as the sharpest cleaver,
explaining the heart of Emerson,
the mind of Thoreau.
You also taught us a composition course,
using Tolstoy's *Anna Karenina* as a model
of good writing.
You never boasted that you could speak Russian.
Someone told me you knew the language.
You wrote a book about the greatness
of Whitman and Dostoevsky.

Being a dull student,
I did not learn as much as I could have
from your courses in my college days.
So now I open your books
in my room
here in my home country far
some forty years after I was in your classes
and try to learn what I missed to learn
about the spirit of the American people,
about the grandeur and beauty of American literature.

YOU DON'T KNOW HOW MUCH I OWE YOU
For Prof. Theodore G. Standing's 83rd Birthday

Your voice was always calm and pleasant,
And your eyes always gentle in the classroom,
As you explained the points good and bad
Of different societies in the world.

Coming from a tiny island, thirty miles around,
Whose tallest mountain is only 700 feet high,
I never fit well in the great country of yours,
Feeling ever insecure, afraid, and frustrated.

And, the happy, friendly atmosphere
Of your home filled my heart with love.
The fresh smell of Mrs. Standing's coffee,
The taste of her scrambled eggs I remember.

Your balanced view of different cultures
Helped me to find myself in a culture new,
And the sense of trust I got at your home
Sustained me till the day of my graduation.

ALL THE POEMS I HAVE WRITTEN I OWE YOU
For Miss Vivian C. Hopkins

Totally lost
in a totally different culture,
I often took refuge
in your office,
pretending to ask you some questions
about your English class.
Sometimes I showed you my translations
of some ancient Japanese poems
which I had worked out
from time to time.
Then, you once told me to write poetry.
So I tried.
I once saw a most splendid full moon
hanging over Saranac Lake
in the summer of 1953, where I had a job washing dishes,
and I tried to write a poem about the full moon,
which turned out rather good.
Ever since that time, I have been writing hundreds of poems,
faithfully following your suggestion
all these 46 years now.
All the poems I have written
I owe you.
All the joy of having some of my poems reprinted
in literature textbook anthologies
in the U.S.A., Canada, Australia and South Africa
I owe you.
All the poems I will have written in my lifetime
I owe you.
You've made a poet
out of a dull, clumsy, maladjusted boy
from the other side of the Pacific Ocean.

(May 4, 1999)

A POEM FOR MRS. KENKICHI MASAI

Mr. Masai and you took me
to a Chinatown restaurant,
the night I arrived
in December 1950.
You would cook the most delicious spaghetti for me
when I returned from Albany.
Mr. Masai and you drove up
all the way to Albany from Maspeth, Long Island
to see me graduate from college
on June 13, 1954.
When my wife and I visited America in 1969,
Mr. Masai and you took us
to the Statue of Liberty,
to the Empire State Building,
to the show at Radio City Music Hall,
to blowfish fishing by Long Island's shore,
to Huntington Mall for shopping.
The ferry boat ride to the Statue of Liberty
was most delightful,
caressed by spring breezes and the warm sun.
Our talks at your kitchen table were fun
at breakfast, lunch, and dinner.
In my August 1981 visit to New York,
you once took me
to the banquet of the Sons of Italy
held at Huntington's Town House,
and I was the only Japanese son of Italy.
I think of you with all my love.

TO AN ASTRONOMY PROFESSOR
On hearing Professor Yumi's final lecture

In your lecture hall
an infinite universe
unfolds itself,
and
right in front of the eyes
of your students
slowly spins the Milky Way Galaxy.
Around its center
swings our solar system
in its own rhythm.
Under your direction
we count the moons
of Jupiter
and touch the ring
of Saturn,
and now we ride
on the tail
of your Halley's comet
into the edge
of the twenty-first century.

(March 1986)

THE BEAUTY OF OLD JAPANESE TALES
For Bruce Allen

Abraham Lincoln was a great US president.
Bruce Allen is my important collaborator.
Certainly we enjoyed working together
During the years of our translation project on "Konjaku Monogatari Shu."
Each and every selection of the old Japanese tales
Furnished us challenging but delightful activities,
Gently nudging us to find the most appropriate English words.
Half-appropriate English words won't do.
In working out each and every English phrase and sentence, a
Just, exact, correct combination of words was what we sought.
Knitting a right robe, we gently put it on the Buddhist priest.
Laudable is the charm of each tale.
Magnificent is the rhythm of the medieval Japanese.
Never have I enjoyed myself so immensely
   as I did in translating those
Old 12th century Japanese tales into contemporary English.
Proudly I now hold the book in my hands.
Quite enthralled is the reader's mind by the savors of these tales.
"Robbers Come to a Temple and Steal Its Bell" is a
Story about how a group of clever robbers stole a temple bell.
The tale about the woman whose unrequited love
   turns her into a serpent
Utterly overwhelms today's audience of the Kabuki or the Noh play.
Very famous is another tale known all over the world
   through the movie made by Kurosawa Akira.
Wonderful are these medieval tales of old Japan.
Exquisitely the blind "koto" player captivates the nobleman
   listening in the moonlight.
You could get really inebriated by the gentle flow
   of the fresh English words recast from the medieval Japanese.
Zealously do I begin to dance in the beauty of our delightful book.

MY SCALPEL IS SHARP
For Dr. Bando

The medieval knight felled his foes
in the battlefield
with his sharp, bright, shining sword.
He cut his way through
to glory, honor, and victory.

The chef of our time is equipped
with his sharp-edged cleaver.
He cuts a big chunk of beef
with one, single stroke of his cleaver.

But my scalpel is even sharper
   than the knight's sword,
     sharper than the chef 's cleaver.
My operating table is my battlefield.
I swing my surgical knife
   and plunge it deep into the patient's abdomen,
   opening it wide,
   to cut off any ailing part
        of the stomach,
           the liver,
            the gall bladder,
           the appendix,
              or
           the colon.
Like a dauntless field commander,
I lead my younger surgeons and nurses
in the battleground of my operating table.

TO ROBINSON JEFFERS

I have come all the way
from a country far in the East
across the Pacific
to see your Tor House,
to touch a corner of the bed by the window,
to feel the rocks of your Tower,
to see sea-lions sunbathing,
to watch "night-herons wearing dawn on their wings,"
to gaze at a hawk perched on a rock,
to hear the beautiful, lonely cry of an eagle.

But I know
I cannot see or hear
in my short visit
what you saw and heard in your lifetime.
So I put my hand on a hard, cold rock
in your Tower,
with my eyes closed,
thinking of your powerful hands
that hammered out great poetry
singing of God, nebulae, mammoth,
stone ages, hawks and eagles,
moon and storm and sea,
creating a terrible beauty
with bitter earnestness.

AT CARMEL IN THE SUMMER OF 1981

From Normandy Inn where I am staying
I walk down Ocean Avenue
and sit on the sandy beach,
listening to the continual sound
of the surges coming in
over and over against the sands,
listening to the sound
Jeffers heard.
This must be the beach
where he and his dog Haig joyously ran
in many an evening half a century ago.
From where I sit
I see no night-herons, nor sea-lions
at this hour of the day,
but this must be the beach he walked along
on his way to watch his sea-lions.
In my boyhood
I often stood
on the hilltop of my home island,
looking east at the grand curvature
of the Pacific, dreaming of a world far beyond the sea.
And now I "look west at the hill of water,"
as Jeffers did,
looking at the huge "eyeball" that stares
into the vast expanse
of the infinite skies.

ON READING "SUMMER'S ARRIVAL" BY LINDA C. GRAZULIS

The summer 2015 issue of *Poems of the World* arrived
At my home in the Far East on December 10.

The poem, "Summer's Arrival" fills my heart with "sunshine,
Azure blue skies, a spread of dandelions and wildflowers,"

When the gingko trees and persimmon trees have all shed
Their leaves in the park nearby.

My ears can hear the "melody of a robin" of America,
When bush warblers are silent in the bushes here.

My soul is filled with the beauty of nature
And begins to "praise God for this season of loveliness."

The poem brings a bright summer of America
To a Japanese looking at his leafless wisteria.

A poet is a special agent
Revealing his or her God to a Shinto reader.

MY WIFE'S COUSIN WAS A NAVY PILOT
——*For Marjorie Thompson Sims*——

My wife's cousin was a navy pilot and took part in the sneak attack on Pearl
Harbor.
He safely returned from the attack and kept on fighting for his country,
And he finally lost his life in the Battle of Midway. .

His country gave him some kind of medal, not a Purple Heart,
But his lost life could never been brought back. Some people try
To glorify the dead soldiers' dedication, but only grief remains.

My elder brother too was sent to the War. His country couldn't send
Enough supplies of food, ammunition, and medicine to the fronts,
And so, he was starved, got sick, and died in New Guinea.

The government took every young man from every family.
Many soldiers were sent to China, Indonesia, the Philippines,
And many other parts of the Southeast of Asia.

No matter how much respect the politicians might try to pay
To the souls that are supposed to be enshrined at Yasukuni Shrine,
None of the souls could approve of the hardships they had gone through.

There has never been a good war in human history. No Japanese can justify
What their soldiers had done in China, the Philippines, and other lands.
No Americans can ever justify the Iraq War that had been started so willfully,

And the A-Bombs so heartlessly dropped on Hiroshima and Nagasaki,
No matter how hard and how cleverly they might try.
So, let's all repent of all the past wrongs that have been committed in wars.

All the countries on Earth should abolish all the nuclear weapons by any means.
All the countries on Earth should refrain from carrying out a preemptive strike.
That is the only way that humans, nay, all the living things, can remain alive.

A HOUSE-DOG'S MONOLOGUE

My master walks me

once a day

toward evening,

my happiest time,

too precious

for me

to walk slow like a fool,

so I run

and run

like a lump of joy,

like a lump of energy,

pulling,

pulling my master

with all my dogged force

along the fence

of the wooded park.

I don't care

even if he has a backache.

Only once in a while

I stop

to growl

at a stray cat

on the other side

of the fence.

A POET TALKING TO HIMSELF
At Amami Airport

To reach the bottom
of your subconscious
you should sit
at the table by the window
in the airport restaurant
of this neighboring island
facing your own island on the horizon,
and sip
some draft beer from the mug,
and get drunk a bit
with the beer,
and get drunk a bit
with memories
of your childhood,
gazing on your home island.
Then you will get to the bottom
of your subconscious,
remembering the tall, tall cumulonimbus
that you saw
on the island
a long, long time ago.

A LITTLE GIRL

A little girl about a year and a half old
Is walking happily
In front of her Mom.
Yes, she is walking happily
In front of her Mom,
Wearing cute pinkish panties.
As I look a bit carefully,
I see her panties are a little swollen
In the middle.
Then I realize her panties are swollen
With a diaper.
The little girl is walking happily
In front of her Mom,
Wearing her cute pinkish panties a little swollen
With a diaper.

THIS SILENT NIGHT
To Franz Gruber

The beautiful music that rolled out
From your solemn organ
More than a century and a half ago
Has kept filling
The hearts of human beings
With peace, happiness and boundless joy.

The world now is bleak and void of love
And many are the acts
Of violence
And our aching hearts need the healing power
Of your immortal song.

Tonight I will do nothing
But play the tune you have worked out,
On the organ in my living room
And fill my heart
With the beauty your soul has caught.

PLAYING "DONAUWELLEN WALZER" ON THE ORGAN

As each of my fingers
fumbled for a right key
a jumble of disconnected sounds
came out
from the scrupulous instrument
    which makes no quick sound
        for a slow touch
        no bold sound
        for a timid touch

but now
after a few weeks
of hard, patient practice
a dancing melody
comes out
    not trickling from the thin fin-
    ger-tips of my hands
but gushing out loud and bold
magnificently
right out of the deep, great, pulsing heart
of Ivanovici

MY GRANDFATHER

My grandfather,
who had lived ninety-four full, long years
on the island,
whose shoulders were broad,
whose arms were big and strong,
who drove his horse,
plowing his small, hard, rocky farms
on the hill
under the scorching island sun
with his sun-tanned body half-naked,
whose spirit no violent typhoons
nor untimely family deaths could bow down,
has been at rest
in our family tomb
at the foot of the hill
for more than thirty years now,

but he would jump to his fleshless feet
and stamp
and raise his bony arms
and clench his toothless jaws
and stare at me
from the depth of his dark eyeholes
and then howl and spit
with his tongueless mouth
as mad as he could be,
if he saw me sneaking
like a faint-hearted hare
in the corner of the world
      afraid of people…
        afraid of winds and hailstones…

GRAVITATION

The Moon revolves about the Earth;
Twelve satellites move about Jupiter,
Which in turn circles the Sun
In a vast orbit. Thus, in the sky
Lesser bodies go round larger ones,
According to the laws of motion
And gravitation.

But, such has not been the case
Here in my home recently.
The new-born daughter is
The gravitational center of happiness,
About which move larger members
Of the joy-filled family.

ONE MONTH OLD DAUGHTER

How have you learned
To smile so sweetly
In the brief period
Of one month?
Your father does not smile
So broadly;
Your mother does not smile
So sweetly.
How have you learned, then,
To smile so sweetly?

Awake from a night's sweet sleep
Your soft face is
As fresh and bright
As the morning.

As your tiny toothless mouth
Broadly unfolds
In the innocent morning joy,
The whole home is filled rich
With delight.

EXPLORATION

Off the infant crawls
Out of the cotton mattress bed,
As the light of the morning sun
Whitens the windows.

She now launches on her venture
Of exploration
Over the floor,
Ever reaching out
For whatever comes into her sight…
The paper,
The yard stick,
Or the abacus.

Here another day begins
For the curious infant
To reach out for sound, for sight,
And for touch,
New,
Unquenchably new.

MY SECRETARY

The one year old girl,
Busy-handed,
Stretches out her mischievous hands
To everything that she can see.
And yet, she is not without her preference.
The solid dark typewriter
On my desk
Is what she likes best.

The clicks and motions
Of the dark magic machine
Amuse her curious eyes,
Ears and hands.
Yes, she is my secretary,
So very efficient
As to press five keys at a time,
Climbing over the typewriter.

SMALL GIRL AND UNIVERSE

I

The little girl does not know
The word "moon."
She calls it "Oh-oh,"
Since it is a wonder
To her curious eyes.

The little girl does not know
The word "airplane."
She calls it "boom-boom,"
Since it "booms"
To her curious ears.

Starting with such basic sounds,
She now begins
To confer a "real" name
Upon everything
That she can see and hear.

II

As the 16-month-old girl calls, "Oh-oh,"
Pointing at something above
With her plum tiny hand,
Her father extends his eyes
From the tip of her hand
Up and up
Through the leafless branches
Of the persimmon tree
And over the tin roof
Of the farm house.

There he finds the moon,
Cool
And beautiful.

Before the word "moon" is learned,
Its beauty is felt,
Keen and fresh.

TONIGHT HE IS FIVE

In the darkened dining room
Five bright flames
Of candles joyfully dance
To the happy birthday song;
The small boy needs not know

What the world has in store
For his future days;
He only needs to joyfully smile
And clap his eager hands,
Looked upon fondly by his folks all.

AT THE END OF SUMMER HOLIDAYS

Children from the mainland city
Who spent their summer
On their grandma's island
Have now flown away
Over the sky far beyond the high, bright-white clouds
    Above the island's coral shores
    Leaving their grandma behind
    By the fence of the airport by the sea

Children from the mainland city
    Their skin baked good and dark
        By the strong island summer sun
    Their arms and legs made stout
        By the swims on the ocean waves
        And by wild romping on the wooded hills
    Their lungs cleansed clean
        With the island's purest air
    Their eyes brightened sharp
        By the island's blinding stars
    Their vocabularies "enriched"
        With the island dialect their cousins taught
    Their thirst quenched
        With the cool water of that mountain stream
    They have flown away
        Over the sky far beyond the island's coral shores
            Leaving their grandma behind
                Who began to hum an island folk song
                    With her eyes full of tears
                      Standing by the fence of the airport by the sea

MY ART DEALER—A Parable—
For Elma

I am a nameless painter,
painting one mediocre picture after another.
All other painters look great,
when I see their works
at the galleries I secretly visit.

All the paintings
that other artists have done
look far superior
to anything I have done.
So, I am an inferiority complex incarnate.

When I was about to break all my brushes
and throw away all my oils,
there came my art dealer,
smiling and saying, "Let me take this one
to the gallery.
I'll try to sell it by any means."

So, she took it to the gallery
and displayed it in a most conspicuous spot,
so that all the visitors could see it.
Then, there came a buyer
who took a special interest in my painting.

He looked at it from this angle.
He gazed on it from that angle.
He liked the white of my dogwoods.
He liked the purple of my lilacs,
and finally decided to buy it.

My art dealer managed to sell it
at the gallery,

when everything others painted
looked to me far better than anything
that I've done in my life.

IN AN ART MUSEUM

Let the eloquent guide explain
the wonders of the master's work,
pointing out every single delicate point
of the masterpiece
    that has survived the test of time,
      that may yet survive
        the test of posterity's keener eyes.

Let the visitors admire
the great work of art
as past generations have.

I will walk away
    and go
    alone and hungry
    into wild heath
      where I may sit on a cold stone,

and there
I will dilute the pigments
    with the seething tears of my heart
and paint
    a rainbow of my dream.

ALOHA OE

Mellow is the beautiful melody,
soft as the Hawaiian breeze,
sweet as the sweetest mango of Hawaii,
soothing as moonlight over Waikiki,
comforting,
consoling,
to the human heart.

This beautiful tune was played by the band
when American troops embarked
on transports
bound for the battlefront.

This is the first song learned
by those immigrant farmers from China,
from Korea,
from Japan,
from Okinawa,
from the Philippines,
as they toiled
on sugarcane plantations,
on pineapple plantations.

This is the very first song
that captivated the lonely hearts
of those immigrant laborers from China,
from Korea,
from Japan,
from Okinawa,
from the Philippines.
When they were tired out,
they would hum this beautiful song
at night,
thinking of the land they have left.

A MAN WHO DIDN'T BECOME A JUDO CHAMPION

I am blessed with thick bones,
strong arms
and big muscles.
I could have been a world champion
in judo
or wrestling
or the dreadful art of *karate*,
but somehow my mother sent me
to a piano teacher
instead of a judo master.
That's how I happen to sit at the piano now
in this concert hall.
I am perfectly at ease
with my art,
my heart full of confidence
like a world champion.
I am at ease
with any great composer's scores,
for I can bang the piano
with my thick-boned fingers.

THE WORLD CONGRESS OF POETS IN MILAN
1988

I drank Italian wine.
I spoke English
with poets from other lands.
We heard a Tunisian poetess read
her poem in French,
and on our way
to the dinner party
at a restaurant
we met
a band of three Arab street musicians
at the entrance
to the "Galleria,"
and to the Arab music
of the street musicians
I began to dance
my home island's Amami dance.
The Italian onlookers
did exclaim, "Bravo! Bravo!"
and I said, "Thank you,"
in English,
but I did laugh in Japanese.

A POEM WRITTEN IN MEMPHIS
For Chester Rider

Back on my home island
there are many who can dance as well as I.
There are some who can dance
even better than I,
so, I have never been praised on the island
for my dancing.
But you, you praise me so heartily,
                    so wholeheartedly,
                    so enthusiastically
that I feel as if I were the most talented dancer
in the whole world.
I learned it in my childhood
at the village festival
on the island,
prodded by my mother and aunts
more than half a century ago.
And I dance it now in 1995
in front of your admiring eyes
on the floor of the hotel's banquet room
right in your hometown,
Memphis, Tennessee.

EFFICIENT IMPRESARIO

—For Wanda Rider, President of 14th World Congress of Poets, 1995—

You summoned us, poets, from different parts of the world.
You called on me to come
all the way from the western edge of the Pacific
to attend the poets' conference
in Memphis, Tennessee.
So I came
to play the roles you had for me to play.
   I did my poetry readings.
   I conducted the haiku seminar.
   I danced my home island dance.
You were the impresario, we actors under your direction.
First you securely set your headquarters
in the Wilson World Hotel,
and then you contacted Boatmen's Bank of Tennessee,
              the printer,
              the sightseeing bus company,
              the TV station,
              the talented entertainers.
You took us to Elvis Presley's Graceland.
You took us to the Rowan Oak Home of William Faulkner.
You took us to the Hotel Peabody to see the famous ducks.
You called the Memphis Queen Line,
telling them to provide us with the best music band in Memphis,
telling them to give us the most delicious food
in the world.
The evening boat-ride on the Memphis Queen
over the golden surface of the Mississippi
was the golden time of my life.
Yes, the Dixieland Band on the Memphis Queen was superb,
so, I couldn't resist the temptation
to jump right onto the floor
to dance my home island's ethnic dance.
The tempo of their Dixieland was just right
for my solo island dance,

so, I danced and danced
to my heart's content.
Then, I had the joy and honor
of dancing with the lady captain of the Memphis Queen.
I did all this
> to your delight,
> to my own delight,
> to the delight
> of all the participants
> of the magnificent show you produced
> under your skilled direction.

AN AMAMI ISLAND FOLK SINGER
— For Tetsuya Ikeda —

His eyes closed,
the singer tunes his snakeskin samisen,
focusing his attention to his ears and fingers,
like a hawk getting its claws ready
for catching its prey.

As he begins to play the prelude
on his masterly samisen,
he hovers over his entranced audience
like a hawk looking for its prey.

Then, he begins to sing
the superb melody of his home island,
and swoops down,
securely seizing the helpless hearts
of his audience
with his astonishing voice.
The entire audience is mesmerized
completely,
helplessly.

In his soulful singing
and his superb samisen music,
we hear the sound of his home island's ocean waves,
we see his home island's bright moon,
we hear the Swan's wings swishing
high above his home island,
we smell the fragrance of the wild lilies
on his home island's hill,
we savor the sweetness of his ancestors' brown sugar.

EASTERN AND WESTERN SHORES OF THE ISLAND

Those islanders
born in the hamlets
on the island's eastern shores
grew up, greeting the bright sunrise
every morning,
but never having a chance to look at a glorious sunset
in the evening,
because of the tall hills
right behind their hamlets.

Those islanders
born in the hamlets
on the island's western shores
grew up, admiring the glorious sunset
every evening,
but never having a chance to look at the bright sunrise
in the morning,
because of the tall hills
right in front of their hamlets.

Those islanders on the eastern shores say,
"It must be great
to finish a day's work, watching a glorious sunset
every evening,"
envying their cousins
on the western shores.

Those islanders on the western shores say,
"It must be great
to get up, welcoming the bright sunrise
every morning,"
envying their cousins
on the eastern shores.

POETRY IS A MAGIC WAVE

—For John W. Easterling, Kentucky, U.S.A.—

Your kind words for the island poet
gently beat on the shores of Kikaijima,
while tender beams of the island moon shine
on the island where Yukitoshi Mishima was born.

His sisters and brothers on the island
have not expected the waves of the Pacific
to come carrying your gentle voice
from yonder side of the great globe.

Dear Poet John W. Easterling, your words of love
have come all the way from the shores of your land,
and now keep beating on the island shores,
gently whispering your message to all his friends.

Poetry is a heart that is warm.
Poetry is a heart that is gentle.
Poetry is a magic wave that can reach
and touch the Earth's farthest shores.

POWER OF A SMALL ISLAND'S INDIGENOUS LANGUAGE

One afternoon, many, many years ago, around 1953,
When I was a young student at the college
In the capital city of the Empire State,
I was walking along Madison Avenue in Albany.

Then, a big, fierce-looking collie appeared,
Dashing toward me,
Across the wide front yard of someone's home.
It must have noticed my Oriental look.
It must have sniffed some Oriental smell in me.

Quickly I wondered what should I do.
Instantly, I thought of what we kids used to do on the island.
When we were chased by a dog on our way back from school,
We would bend over,
Pretending to pick up and throw a rock.
Then, the dog would flinch and walk away.

That was exactly what I did,
Bending over and pretending to pick up a rock.
But, of course,
I found no rock on Madison Avenue in Albany,
And I found myself howling,
"Dahrimun! Uchikussarindo!"
It wasn't English.
It wasn't Japanese, either.
It was my sudden shout in my Kikaijima language.
I didn't know what an American would say
Under such circumstances.
What came out from my angry mouth was:
"You, hateful thing! I'll kill you!" in my home island language

Then, threatened by my loud, angry Kikaijima curse,

The big, fierce-looking collie stopped, turned back, and walked away.
But now, Earth's dear, old, indigenous languages are dying out,
Replaced with television languages all over the world.

TO A YOUNG LADY

Do not be like a star,
Shining ever
From afar
Beyond my reach.

Be like a flower,
Smiling ever
From a garden near
Within my reach.

TO A COUSIN ON THE ISLAND
For Katsuhiko Koriyama

While I wandered around from one place to another
like a rootless duckweed,
you have remained on the island,
tilling the land of our ancestors.
Drops of sweat falling down from your chin and elbows
have soaked into the earth of your sugarcane fields,
into which the sweat of our ancestors had soaked.
You have lived under the bright moon and stars
of the island our ancestors had watched
over countless generations.
You have endured the violent typhoons
which often rage over the island,
uprooting the crops and vegetables.
You hear the sound of the waves of the ocean
at midnight
that keep beating
on the island shores.
Living in a city of the mainland,
I often think of the days
when we swam together like dolphins in our childhood
chasing fish around the coral reefs.
I often think of you
now keeping a small island village store
by the seashore looking over the sea.

AT THE CONCERT HALL
—For Masayuki Kurata—

The singer holds
The edge of the grand piano,
Taking deep breaths,
With his eyes closed,
Trying to calm his inner tensions,
Facing the imminent moment
Of breaking the silence of the hushed hall,
While the lady accompanist silently awaits
The critical moment
When the singer will get ready
To start his art.

Now the singer opens his eyes
As if awakening from a trance
And gently sends a signal.
The pianist responds
With a smiling nod
And begins to touch the keys of her piano
With her masterly hands,
Urging the singer
To start his song,
And now the concert hall is gradually filled
With the music of Franz Schubert singing
His timeless serenade to the whole world
In a most beautiful voice.

A LOVE SONG JUST FOR YOU

Millions and millions of men
Have sung
Millions and millions of songs
Since the beginning of time
In praise of love,
In praise of their attractive women.
Standing on a hill,
Sitting by a lakeshore,
Watching the sea,
Looking at the moon and stars,
They sang,
They sang songs of love.

When I think
Of all the great songs
That all the great poets have sung,
I hesitate,
I mumble.
It seems impossible for me
To sing a song as great as their songs.

But when I think
Of your beauty and my love for you,
I boldly take up a pen
In my hand
To write a song,
A song just for you.

A MORNING SONG

When I go to bed
I always put a notebook
at my bedside
so that
I may depict
your beauty
when I see you
in my dream.

Groping in the dark,
I scribble
and scratch
word by word
recording my joy
of seeing you.

In the morning
I see strange loops
and crooked lines
like wanton tracks
of creeping earthworms
on the open pages
of the notebook.

As I sit
at my typewriter
deciphering the illegible scrawls,
loop by irregular loop,
line by crooked line,
your smiling face
begins to appear
right in front of my eyes.

TO MY YOUNG GODDESS

Coming out of the sushi bar,
we walked together
to a street corner,
and there we stood together
for a while.
From there
you could have walked
straight to the subway station,
heading for home,
but instead you said,
"I would like to walk with you
for a while,"
and so we walked along together
side by side,
and then you said,
"I'm happy
I was able to see you tonight."
With such sweetness
you filled my heart with love
and happiness.
You are my young goddess,
fondly enshrined
in the altar
of my heart.

ABOARD AN OCEAN LINER

As the swan-like ocean liner
gracefully glided
over the sea
over the blue, wide, wide open sea
we stood together
upon the gently swaying promenade deck

deftly the camera has caught
the happiest moment
of the happy voyage
the bright smile in your eyes
the sweet sea breeze in your hair

and now I look back
upon this irrecoverable moment
in the endless flow of eternity
feeling the softness of your arms
in my heart

A HYMN TO MY LADY

I insert a sheet
of paper
into my typewriter

and begin to compose
a hymn for you. What's the use

of my art
but to record
the beauty of your eyes?

When you receive
this song of mine,
hug it tight

on your warm breasts
and kiss it
with your tender lips.

AN ARTIST'S APOLOGY TO HIS DAUGHTER

You may feel uncomfortable,
looking at those paintings
of nude women
your father has painted.
He did look at the women
as intensely
as he could, trying to reproduce
the gentle curves of their breasts.
He counted the threads of a model's hair
hanging on her nape.
He could feel the heartbeat
of the women in front,
as he moved his brush on the canvas.
Perhaps he loved these women
more strongly than he loved your mother.
Here they are, painted for ages to come,
exposing their naked bodies
to the sun.

FANTASIA EROTICA

As a village maiden
bathes alone
in the golden moonlight
stark-naked
under a silvery waterfall
at the foot
of the island hill
the stream of water
presses its cool lips
tight against her burning lips
and then
it begins to softly knead
her rich breasts
round and round
admiring the strawberry nipples
and then massages her supple thighs
driving her wild
with ecstasy
her dazed eyes
glancing up
at the stars above
that are peeping
breathlessly
through the swaying meshes
of bamboo leaves
in the magic music far
of the eternal sea

6.8 BILLION HUMAN BEINGS PRAYED FOR YOU
For the Brave Chilean Miners

6.8 billion human beings,
the entire population
of the world prayed for you,
you, 33 miners,
trapped at San Jose mine near Copiano, Chile.
People from Alaska to Zimbabwe,
people from Zambia to Alabama,
all the human beings living on Earth peered at you
trapped in the mine 700 meters below the ground,
watched the rescue work,
holding their breath,
praying for your safe return
to the surface of the Earth.

You had stayed there alive,
stayed there alive and sane,
yes, stayed there alive and sane,
sustained by your unflinching will to live
at the bottom of the Earth,
700 meters below the ground.

What if some had panicked?
What if some had started a fight?
Under the strong, sagacious, superb leadership
of Luis Urzua,
you were divided into three groups.
You remained organized.
You didn't panic.
You are the bravest lot of men
in human history.
This certainly is one of the most laudable feats
that has ever been made
in the history of mankind.

THE MOST WONDERFUL EVENING IN MY LIFE
On the Occasion of the World Congress of Poets in China in 2005

On the evening of November 5, 2005
The Chinese bus driver did us drive
To a fine restaurant in the suburb
Of Beijin, which did look good and superb.
Speeches were aye given by Dr. Fan,
The congress president from Taiwan,
Mr. Yuzon, the head of our poetry group,
The white-haired Dame Lee who didn't stoop
To her advanced age of 100,
And some Chinese poets who devoted
Themselves to hosting the world poetry meeting.
The Chinese poet, Mr. Nan's greeting
Was friendly with all his smiling face.
With friendship we each other did embrace.
We had good foods, plenty of beer and wine.
The atmosphere of the banquet was just fine.
Then a band of Chinese musicians began
To play. "Peace and Friendship" was our slogan.
After all the drinking, I had to go
To the Men's Room and then I returned to
The merry room of our restaurant.
I felt an irresistible urge instant
To start dancing my dear home island's dance.
Dancing toward the stage, I took a glance
At all the poets at tables and white-attired cooks
Who were all smiles and had amazed looks.
They were all taken by surprise and delight.
Their surprised, happy eyes were shining bright.
The cooks in the kitchen all stopped working,
Completely enthralled by my dancing.
While dancing, I extended my right hand
To shake hands with each of the cooks of that land.
Even the 100-year-old Dame Lee
Was swaying her aged body in glee,

Urged by my delightful, rhythmical dance.
Even the band men all began to dance in a trance.

ON THE GREAT WALL OF CHINA
For Rafael Jesus Gonzalez

On November 3, 2005
My poet-friends started singing
"Happy birthday to you" for me
On the Great Wall of China
At the suggestion of Rafael Jesus Gonzalez.

No sooner had they started singing
For my 79th birthday than I jumped
Right into the middle space of the circle
And began to dance my home island's *Amami* dance.

To their singing, I danced and danced on the Great Wall of China.
"Who has ever celebrated his or her birthday
With happy dancing
On the Great Wall of China?" I now wonder.

AT AGE FOUR SCORE YEARS AND ELEVEN

Living my life on Earth for four score years and eleven,
I now look back at all my main memories in my life.
I was born on a small island, Kikaijima, in the Amami Islands
Between mainland Japan and Okinawa in 1926.
We, kids walked to the primary school barefoot,
And on our way to school, we sometimes saw a flock of dolphins
Rolling and jumping in the ocean right in front of our eyes.
When we kids stood on the hilltop of Kikaijima,
We could see a grand curvature of the Pacific Ocean,
Showing us that the Earth is round.
In 1941, I went on to Kagoshima Normal School in mainland Japan.
In December 1941 the Japanese navy attacked Pearl Harbor.
My wife's cousin was a navy pilot and took part in the attack.
The war Japan had started was most horrifying.
And what did the Japanese soldiers do in China in 1930s and 1940s?
And in other parts of Asia until the war's end in 1945?
Have we Japanese apologized to Chinese and other Asians sincerely?
On April 1, 1945 the U.S. forces landed on Okinawa,
Thus, bloody ground battles were fought on Okinawa.
On August 6, 1945 the first atomic bomb was dropped on Hiroshima
For the first time in human history.
And on August 9, another atomic bomb was dropped on Nagasaki.
The war formally came to an end on August 15, 1945.
And on February 2, 1946, the Amami Islands were cut off from Japan
Together with all the other islands in the Ryukyu chain.
We could go to Okinawa freely, but not to Japan.
So I went to Okinawa Foreign Language School in 1948,
And there I studied English like mad, furiously,
Reading old issues of the *Reader's Digest* which U.S G.I.s gave away.
Then, I worked at Kadena Airbase as an interpreter in 1949,
And then at the Ryukyu Military Government as a translator.
Fifty-two young people were selected and sent
To U.S. colleges and universities in 1950, and I was one of them.
I studies at the University of New Mexico 1950-51.

Then, I transferred to the New York State College
For Teachers at Albany, and studied there 1951-54.
There my English teacher, Miss Vivian C. Hopkins suggested
That I write poetry in English.
That's how I got started to write poetry in English, not in Japanese.
I first submitted one of my early poems, "Cave Man's Moonrise" in 1954
To *The Christian Science Monitor*, which they accepted.
"Unfolding Bud" they printed in 1957 is one of my best-loved poems.
I used to submit poems to *Poetry Nippon* and *The Mainichi Daily News*,
But they are no longer published. *The Japan Times* doesn't print poetry.
Of all the poems I have written, eight have been reprinted
In 26 or 27 school textbooks in America, Canada, Australia, and South Africa.
Some of my poems have been translated into Chinese, Greek, Korean, Italian,
Vietnamese, Arabic, and some other languages, according to the Internet.
And then, in1997, I met Elma, the editor of *Poems of the World*,
At a poetry conference, "The World Congress of Poets" held in England.
And ever since that time, I've been submitting my poems
To *Poems of the World*, a wonderful poetry magazine in the world.
"Lines about the Atomic Bombs" by a Japanese poet, Kyutai Tsuchiya
In the Summer 2017 issue of *Poems of the World*
Is the most powerful poem about the atomic bombs ever written in the world,
And of all the numerous translations I have made into English,
"Lines about the Atomic Bombs" is the best, the most successful translation.
Of the years allotted to me, four score and eleven years will not come again,
And so, in the autumn of my life on Earth, I fondly think
Of all the beautiful, excellent, powerful, superb "poems of the world."
And I feel proud of the wonderful work our editor has been doing.
In the autumn of my life I plan to bear some more bright-red mellow persimmons.

130ᵀᴴ ANNIVERSARY OF TOYO UNIVERSITY

Enryou Inoue founded *Tetsugakukan*—The Academy of Philosophy—
At Tatsuoka-cho in Tokyo's Hongo district in September 1887,
Advocating his belief, "The basis of all learnings lies in philosophy."
He moved the school to the present site of Hakusan in 1897.

This uphill road to the campus we walk along now
Is the same road which all the former students walked up,
Wearing their *hakama* trousers, loudly clattering their clogs
Until around the 1930s.

The old Hall Number Five stood on Hakusan Hill till the 1960s.
The façade of old Hall Number Five reverentially held the reliefs
Of the four greatest sages of the world,
Confucius, Buddha, Socrates and Kant.

The old library was a modest building, covered with ivy vines.
A tall paulownia tree nearby used to bear purple blossoms in season.
And there stood the old University Auditorium a little way off,
Where enrollment ceremonies and commencements were held.

In the passage of one century plus 30 years,
Toyo University has evolved through many changes,
Replacing dear old buildings with new structures,
Rearranging academic and administrative systems.

We joyously celebrated the centennial in 1987.
The then president Koichi Kansaku started a contest to publish
One Hundred Tanka by Young Students Today as a memorial project,
And now it receives about 50,000 entries every year.

In baseball, the Matsunuma brothers as fine pitchers,
Mitsuo Tatsukawa, a fine catcher, and others played well.
In the finals of Toto 6 Baseball League or All-Japan University Baseball League,
Our College Anthem shook the Meiji Shrine Baseball Stadium.

In 2009 our Hakone Relay Road Race Team won the race
For the first time ever in the history of Toyo University.
Ryuji Kashiwabara ran his uphill course in an amazing time,
Thus helping the team win the memorable first win.

In the London Olympics, Ryota Murata won the gold medal
In the middleweight class in boxing.
In the Rio de Janeiro Olympics, Kosuke Hagino won the gold medal
In the men's 400-meter individual medley in a time of 4 minutes, 6.5 seconds.

In the men's 4x100-meter relay, Yoshihide Kiryu
Of Toyo University was the third runner
In the four-man team of Japan, which won the silver medal,
In a time of 37.60 seconds; next only to Bolt's Jamaica team.

And on Saturday, September 9, 2017,
Yoshihide Kiryu broke the wall of 10 seconds
Of men's 100 meters with the time of 9.98 seconds
For the first time in the history of our country.

We are also proud of our university's academic activities
In the fields of literature and philosophy
Of India, China, and Japan.
Achievements are remarkable in other fields, too.

Like Underground Water: The Poetry of Mid-Twentieth Century Japan,
An excellent anthology of translated modern poetry of Japan
And *Japanese Tales from Times Past*, a new translation
From *"Konjaku Monogatari Shu,"* are the happy outcomes of my work at Toyo.

In the history of the institute, Toyo University has accepted students
From all over the world, sending them back as graduates.
And the first overseas branch of our Alumni Association
Has been opened in Shanghai, one of the greatest cities of the world.

We have dozens of sister schools all over the world,
Exchanging researchers with each other,

Exchanging results of research work with each other,
As friendly collaborators, not as competitive rivals.

Now, in the year 2017, we are proudly celebrating the 130th anniversary
Of Toyo University's founding.
And each of us is contributing something
To the ceaseless development of Toyo University.

In the year 2018, on February 26, in the Tokyo Marathon,
Yuta Shitara established a new Japanese record: 2: 6:11.
Now, he is off to a good start for the Tokyo Olympics 2020.
Toyo University is ever on its way to a bright future.

JETLINER

now he takes his mark
at the very farthest end of the runway
looking straight ahead , eager, intense
with his sharp eyes shining

he takes a deep, deep breath
with his powerful lungs
expanding his massive chest
his burning heart beating like thunders

then…after a few…tense moments…of pondering
he roars at his utmost
and slowly begins to jog
kicking the dark earth hard
and now he begins to run
kicking the dark earth harder
then he dashes, dashes like mad, like mad
howling, shouting, screaming, and roaring

then with a most violent kick
he shakes off the earth's pull
softly lifting himself into the air
soaring higher and higher and higher still
piercing the sea of clouds
up into the chandelier of stars

LIKE A STATELY GIANT EAGLE

like a stately giant eagle
approaching its perch
the huge four-engine jet
gradually descends
to land
steadily slowing down
slowing down
its stupendous speed
by mightily pushing down the air
with its widespread wings
ever restraining
its fast beating heart
consciously…
muffling its prodigious roars
deep down its throat
the huge jet
comes down
and down with its eyes
firmly fixed on the goal
with all its heavy claws out
ready
to catch
catch the mark

A JET LANDING IN CLOUDS

In the thick clouds
Overhead
I cannot see
anything whatever
but only hear
the loud roars
of a huge eagle of metal
descending
in total invisibility
feeling out
its way
carefully
all its magic senses
fully alert
breathlessly focused
on the call
from the ground
through
the thick veil
of the evening rain

JETLINER UP IN THE STRATSPHERE

making a ceaseless, tireless hissing sound
up in the highest sky
the wide-opened air-intakes
of the gigantic jetliner
keep on sucking in
the thin, clean, freezing air
deep into the mighty lungs

inhaling, compressing, burning the purest air
in the powerful lungs
the jetliner continuously spits out
the violent jet of heated breath
driving its massive body
on the wide-spread shining wings
high above the night-covered earth

its glaring eyes
in the utter dark of night are sharply set
to a far, far, distant point
beyond the immense heaving sea

while a baby sleeps sweetly
holding its half-finished bottle
on its loving mother's lap
the stupendous roaring jetliner
darts
sailing among the naked stars

SONG OF A JET PILOT

Now, we will make a long, long flight
    Over the ocean, over the frozen northern sea
    Over snow-capped mountains
    High above rolling hills and smog-veiled cities
All the way far…to the other side of the globe

My gigantic metallic eagle
    Crouches at the starting point on the runway
    Ready to dash and soar and race with the stars
I try to calm my pounding heart
    Holding the control lever, tight and tense

As I slowly release the brakes
    The stupendous, bullet-shaped jetliner begins to dash
    With all its mighty engines fully open
    Violently exerting their maximum power

Cleaving the darkness of night
        Shaking the entire earth awake
        My jetliner speeds like a space rocket
        And begins to race ah! with shooting stars

THE PLANE'S SHADOW

As our plane flew
away from the island
over the sea,
I caught sight of its shadow
on the surface of the sea.
As the plane made its approach
to the airport
on the neighboring island,
the shadow came nearer and nearer,
becoming larger and larger,
skimming the surface of the sea,
and then the shadow
became just as large as the plane,
and over the runway,
after racing with the plane for a while,
the shadow caught the plane
with its open arms
safe
at an exact moment.

SONG OF A LOCAL AIRLINE'S PILOT

Let the huge B747 roar
with its powerful engines fully open
36,000 feet above the earth
at the speed of 600 miles an hour
across the Pacific Ocean nonstop
over to the other side of the earth,
but I will let my humble 19-seat plane drone
from a small island
to another
at 200 miles an hour
only 1,500 feet above the East China Sea.
One of my air routes
is perhaps the shortest in the world,
only a-seven-minute flight.
Let the huge B747 race
with a spaceship or a UFO,
hurtling among the naked stars,
but I will let the shadow of my plane race
with a dolphin
over the surface of the blue sea.
My only companion
is my copilot sitting by me,
no smiling stewardesses at all.
But my landing skill is so good,
none of my passengers can ever feel
the landing gear touch the ground.
Let the captain of the huge B747 land his plane
on a magnificent airport
on the other side of the earth.
I will bring my plane to a stop
right in front of the one-story airport building
and let my passengers see
their cousins and friends
just looking through the windows.

I FEEL LIKE AN ASTRONAUT

Of cause, I haven't ridden on the space shuttle.
I have only watched it launched
with the most powerful rockets
on television
soaring, roaring, darting, zooming,
up into limitless space
on its wondrous mission.

Today I ride a high-speed pleasure boat
on Lake Tazawa
in northern Japan
at nine in the morning,
the first boat of the day.

Leaving the quay,
the 19-ton high-speed boat soon starts going
at its maximum speed.
Standing by its starboard,
I watch it spurting a powerful jet of water.
The bow of the boat is cleaving the surface
of the lake
madly,
crazily,
yet so smoothly.

The thrilling sense of speed I feel
aboard the small high-speed pleasure boat
is more than I can describe in words.
I feel like an astronaut,
while the boat dashes on,
roaring, darting, zooming,
over the blue beautiful lake
in northern Japan
in the early summer of 2010.

THE LAST MINUTE CHECK
At an Island Airport

Before climbing up
into the cockpit
the captain and his copilot
fondly pat
on the surface
of their plane's body,
and kick
the thick black tires
of the landing gear
and turn the propellers
with their hands
round and round
for a few times
to see
if everything is well
with their plane
before soaring
on its powerful wings
up
into the sky.

A GLIMPSE OF THE BRIDGE

Like a jetliner
cleaving its way
through
thick white clouds
up in the sky
the golden gate bridge
cleaves its way
through
drifting fog
across the bay
now appearing
now disappearing

SECTION 6

ONE OF THFE MOST POWERFUL EARTHQUAKES

One of the most powerful earthquakes
in the history of Japan
hit northeastern Japan
at 2:46 p.m.,
on March 11, 2011.
Its magnitude was 9.0, the strongest ever recorded in Japan.
Thousands of houses, stores, hospitals, offices,
all kinds of buildings were destroyed.
And the tsunami caused by the earthquake was even more devastating
than the quake itself.
Countless cars, tens of thousands of human beings
together with their houses and buildings were all washed away
by the furious, raging waves
of the angry sea,
destructive,
shattering,
merciless,
cruel.

Look at the black tides surging in!
Listen to the sounds of things swallowed by the wild waves!
Strangely enough, people are too horrified to scream.
Earth instantly has changed into Hell.
This is the power of nature.

HUMANS ARE HELPLESS AGAINST NATURE'S POWER

Egyptians built Pyramids with enormous rocks
4,500 years ago.
Greeks built the beautiful Parthenon
with shining marble
in the first half of the first century B.C..
Americans built the soaring Empire State Building
with steel and concrete
in 1931.
Humans can fly to the moon.
Humans can connect continents
with stupendous bridges.
Humans can make beautiful music,
can paint gorgeous paintings,
can sing and dance marvelously.

But they are helpless
when they are hit by a big earthquake and tsunami.

Humans invented powerful nuclear bombs.
But earthquakes are
much more powerful than any atomic bomb.
An earthquake can shake the earth more powerfully
than any atomic bomb.
An atomic bomb can destroy an entire city,
but a tsunami can push billions of billions of tons of seawaters
with its incredible energy,
washing away thousands of houses, cars, boats, and helpless humans.
No single atomic bomb can ever destroy hundreds of cities,
towns, and villages
like a tsunami can.
Humans are helpless
when nature hits them with its unimaginable energy.

THE INCREDIBLE POWER OF THE TSUNAMI

The incredibly powerful tsunami came roiling,
triggered by the strongest earthquake;
tens of thousands of humans perished
in the black, violent, wild, mad, whirling waves.

The overwhelming tsunami was caused by the powerful earthquake.
It came attacking the cities,
towns, villages where human beings had lived
for many generations
in the land of their ancestors.

The tsunami came, driving incredible masses of black seawaters,
swallowing houses, cars, and humans,
gulping them all down,
roiling madly,
ruthlessly,
violently,
and so mercilessly.

Oh, the incredible power of the tsunami
that hit northeastern Japan
on March 11, 2011
was as shocking as that September 11!

That September 11 hit New York and Washington,
shocking human consciousness
as never before.

The March 11 quake hit northeastern Japan,
shocking the consciousness of us Japanese
as never before.

Tens of thousands of people perished,
and tens of thousands of people lost their families and houses.

WHEN HUMANS ARE IN A CRISIS

When tens of thousands of people were hit
by the great earthquake,
the overwhelming tsunami,
and the unprecedented nuclear plant's disasters,
rescue teams arrived
from many countries of the Earth,
to save the suffering victims.

Here human beings worked together
with all their might
to save the victims of the great earthquake,
the overwhelming tsunami,
and the unprecedented nuclear disasters.

Human beings can be enemies to each other,
hating each other,
fighting each other,
killing each other,
but
they can also be helpful friends,
working together,
helping each other,
with friendship,
with compassion,
with benevolent hearts,
at a time of a great crisis.

ONE WEEK AGO TODAY

On Friday, March 11, 2011
the huge earthquake hit northeastern Japan
and the tsunami caused by it
destroyed countless families, homes, jobs,
cars, farms, tractors, everything.
The entire seacoasts were swallowed,
flooded,
washed away.

And tonight,
one week later,
on Friday March 18, 2011,
the moon is full and beautiful,
as if nothing had happened
one week ago today,
on Friday, March 11, 2011.

We know nothing about the mechanism,
the intention,
the will,
or the desire,
of Great Nature.

And the moon is shining bright and beautiful,
as if nothing had happened
one week ago today,
on Friday, March 11, 2011.

HOW WONDERFUL IT IS JUST TO BE ALIVE!

So many people perished.
So many people lost their families.
So many people lost their homes.
So many people were washed away
by the roiling waves of the tsunami.
So many people looked for their families in vain.

And looking at them on television,
I realize nothing is more precious than just being alive.
I firmly make up my mind:
I'll never complain
about anything in my life
from now on.

What a wonderful thing it is
to ride a bicycle to the station newsstand
just to buy a sports paper,
or to the convenience store
just to buy a weekly magazine.
How wonderful it is
to stop by someone else's hedge to smell the fragrant daphne!
How wonderful it is
to stop by someone else's garden to admire plum blossoms!
Oh, what a wonderful thing it is
just to be alive and view the bright, beautiful moon shining in the sky!
The morning sun gives light and heat
even to a humble person like me. How wonderful it is
just to be alive, breathing the fresh morning air!

SECTION 7

I COULD GO STRAIGHT HOME

I could go straight home
To see the seven o'clock news
In time, but I walk slowly
Along the road
By the wooded park.
The bright Moon is overhead
And the big, bright Venus is shining
In the western sky.
I would rather enjoy my leisurely walk
By the park,
Admiring the Moon and the Evening Star
Than hurrying home
To watch the seven o'clock news
Full of news about fighting and explosions
In Iraq.
They say the world is unstable
And full of dangers of terrorist attacks,
But who has made the world unstable?
Who indeed?

OF COURSE I WANT TO SING A SONG

Of course I want to sing a song
About the hydrangeas in bloom,
Standing by the roadside.

Of course I want to keep standing
By the pond in the park,
Watching large carp leisurely swimming.

Of course I want to make a song
About the full moon freshly shining,
As freshly as a million years ago.

Of course I want to keep watching
The brood of spotbill duck chicks
Expressing their joy of just being alive.

But I must cry out loud and curse
The evil of the nuclear power plant
Contaminating the land, sea and sky.

THE SUN SAYS TO MAN

"I have been giving my heat and light to all the planets and their satellites
In my solar system
Ever since the beginning of time.
I have been giving my heat and light to all the animals that have come
And gone on the surface of the Earth.
I have been giving my heat and light to you, Man,
Ever since you came into being on the surface of the Earth.
You didn't freeze to death because of the heat I gave you.
You didn't starve to death because of the food I gave you
Through photosynthesis working with the green leaves of vegetables and grains,
Though I am 149 million km's away.
And now you try to steal energy
Out of the nucleus of the atom of uranium 235
By breaking it for the purpose of making your life comfortable
Ever so greedily,
Ever so selfishly,
Ever so arrogantly.
You should learn to use my limitless energy more efficiently,
Instead of trying to steal energy from the nucleus of the uranium atom
By means of your awkward, immature, poor technology.
Now, your dairy farmers can't sell their milk,
Because it is contaminated with radioactive materials.
Now, your farmers can't sell their vegetables,
Because they are contaminated with radioactive materials.
Now, your fishermen can't sell their catch,
Because it is contaminated with radioactive materials.
Now, hundreds of thousands of people have evacuated their homes.
Why don't you tap the limitless amounts of heat under the ground?
Why don't you tap the limitless amounts of power in the winds?
Why don't you tap the limitless amounts of energy in the waves of the ocean?
You should build solar energy plants all over the Earth
To catch the free, limitless energy I have been sending
Across the distance of 149 million km's."

A NUCLEAR LEGEND

As God stood
by the side
of the milky way,
feeding his bears and lions
he happened to cast a casual glance
at planet earth
and saw
some flashes popping up
like lightning
and no sooner had he known
that nuclear war was on
than he quickly breathed in
all the air in the universe
deep into His enormous lungs
and then breathed it out most violently
to blow off
all the missiles just before they hit their targets
far
over to the other side
of the milky way

NUCLEAR WINTER

If a nuclear war broke out
and hundreds of black mushroom clouds
went up
to the uppermost limits
of the atmosphere,
keeping
all the warm life-giving sunlight
from falling
on the earth,
all the oceans and lakes and rivers
would be deep-frozen
in a day or two
and all the fishes
would be inlaid solid
in the ice as hard as granite
their eyes
looking up into the sunless sky
cursing the folly
of humankind that was smart enough
to invent the nuclear bomb
and foolish enough to use it

CIVILIZATION ADVANCES

Man has succeeded in flying in the sky
just like a bird,
even faster than a hawk or an eagle.
Man has succeeded in sailing the ocean
just like a dolphin,
even faster than a dolphin.
Man has succeeded in diving into deep seas
just like a whale,
even deeper than a whale.
Man has succeeded in making sheep, cows, and pigs
in his laboratory by combining female eggs and cells' nuclei.
Man has succeeded in turning grass-eating cows
into carnivorous animals
by feeding them with powdered bones or powdered meat,
just to speed up their growing.
Cows hate to eat powdered bones or powdered meat,
because it stinks and tastes so bad.
So, they revolted against man
by falling into the mad cow disease
for the first time in the history of Planet Earth.
Man has succeeded in making the most terrible bombs
by splitting the atoms of uranium or fusing the atoms of hydrogen
and he has even used them,
slaughtering hundreds of thousands of lives
with only two bombs in Hiroshima and Nagasaki.
Man succeeded in killing trees and grasses in Vietnam
by spilling a defoliant agent,
thus also damaging reproductive organs
of Vietnamese women
and having deformed babies born.
Is advanced technology making human beings any happier?
When human beings can't take care of a nuclear power plant's disaster,
they want to build more nuclear plants
and even export them to other countries.

THE PERSIAN CORMORANT IN PROTEST

What has happened to my sea?
It is all covered with thick, black, sticky stuff.
It gets in my eyes.
It gets in my nose.
It gets in my bill.
It sticks to my wings.
It has glued all my feathers.
I no longer can fly.
I just totter
along the blackened sandy beach,
until I die
of exhaustion
and starvation.
I curse the blackened sea.
I curse the smoky sky.
I curse the human beings,
as I totter
along the blackened, sticky shore.

NOTHING IS MORE PRECIOUS THAN PEACE
Looking at a Picture Post Card of Ie Island off Okinawa

On the beach of the island
where Japanese soldiers
and invading U.S. marines
fought one of the fiercest battles
in human history
in the spring of 1945,
two island fishermen
are now mending their fishing nets
by their boat
under the bright Okinawan sun.

The sea is crystal blue
and the sand is blindingly white,
as if no human blood had been shed,
the air is clean and pure,
as if no battle smoke had covered up the island,
birds are singing
in the seaside woods,
as if no dying human beings
had writhed and groaned
here
right on this very beach.

BRITISH TROOPS LEAVING SOUTHAMPTON

On Looking at a News-photo on May 14, 1982

Women stand on the pier,
Seeing their sons, husbands, or lovers off,
As they leave
For the Falkland Islands where they will fight.
Some of the women hold their babies
In their arms,
Which have often held their men
In happy embraces.
They stand, shedding bitter tears,
Tears more bitter than blood itself.
These are tears,
Heart-rending tears
That womenfolk have shed
Ever since they saw their men off
To the very first tribal war in human history
On some hillside in the summer sun.
Some of these tearful eyes may never see them back,
The men they see now leaving aboard the ship,
The men they love so much.
Let us hope
That the time will come
When human beings will come to realize
That a woman's man is far heavier
Than the planet itself.

TROOPS LEAVING ABOARD QUEEN ELIZABETH II

On Looking at a May 14, 1982 News-photo

Dear baby boy,
Held in your mommy's arms,
You turn your back
On the newsman's camera.
You turn your tiny back
On the ship your daddy is on.

You don't know
Where your daddy is going,
Nor what fate is awaiting your daddy
At his destination.
You don't know
Why your mommy is crying.

I only pray, dear baby boy,
Your daddy will come back safe,
Crawling through showers of bullets and shells.
I only pray
Your daddy will come back safe
To hug you again,
Just as he did this morning.

REQUIEM TO THE ISLAND HORSES

Many a colt was born
into the bright sunlight
of that small green island,
and they ran and jumped,
madly happy for just being alive,
breathing the cleanest air under the bluest sky,
kicking and trampling the stones and dirt
by the blue, blue sea.
But when they grew,
a black iron ship came from behind the horizon far
to carry them away,
away to a place they knew nothing of,
and there they were bridled by force
and trained to pull heavy, heavy loads.
And they were again carried away,
this time on a much larger ship,
to a place…where fireballs were exploding,
and human beings were killing each other,
which they had not seen nor heard of
on the island where they happily ran.
Those gentle horses pulled the heavy loads
up the mountainsides and down the slopes,
and they got bogged down
in the mud in rain or snow,
and they got tired out
or starved,
or got hit by the enemy bullet right on the head.
They all died,
raising a faint neigh
at the very last moment,
perhaps thinking of the clear, blue sky
of the island where they were born.

ARMAGEDDON AT OUR DOOR

Russian missiles are deployed
Along the borders of Eastern Europe,
With Pershingg-2 missiles to cope,
And we don't want our planet destroyed.

Right in the potato fields of Idaho
And by the coal mines of Siberia
Not far from North Korea,
Silos of missiles are set for the foe.

In the blue sea around Japan
Russian nuclear subs are rampant.
And U.S. flattops too are vigilant.
So I want to flee to Saipan.

Should Mr. Reagan dream a bad dream,
Obsessed by a Russian surprise attack,
Ever ready to make a counterattack,
He might cry, "Push the button!" in a scream.

In a bad dream, Mr. Chernenko might see
Hundreds of U.S. missiles come flying,
The entire sky shaking,
From the other side of the North Sea.

Then he would give his quick order
To his commander in charge
Of the buttons connected to computers large
To launch missiles, the gravest blunder.

What would come to pass
If an American sub exploded accidentally
And one of the missiles flew irretrievably
Over the Pacific to Las Vegas?

Should a Russian missile come loose
From a Russian bomber in a war game
And hit Anchorage, setting the city aflame,
It would shock the Alaskan moose.

Some innocent rats might bite
At the wires of the computer
That might activates the missiles sinister
And throw the world into an all-out fight.

Nuclear war could break out accidentally.
Of course, no one wants it at all,
But the final, horrid day could fall,
Unless man puts away the weapons totally.

The beautiful Siberian eagles
Have nothing to do with communism,
Nor with capitalism,
Nor with any human wrangles.

The happy sea otters of Pacific Grove
Have no use for the SS-20.
Of pleasure and sunlight they have plenty.
Of nuclear war would they disapprove.

All the fish in the sea
And all the beasts on land would curse
The human stupidity, and endorse
No nuclear war, but a happy wild life free.

All the birds in the sky
Happily fly in search of food and mate
And nuclear war they would hate.
Of the East-West distrust they don't know why.

Dear readers, did you enjoy my rhyme
Which appeared on the 13th of December?
I enjoyed writing it myself, as I remember.
It must have brought fun to your breakfast time.

But this present rhyme is grim.
These lines are not bright, but right,
And depict humankind's dire plight.
Now let's go sing a merry Christmas hymn.
                (*Mainichi Daily News*, December 23, 1984)

CONFUSION

When I looked at the earth-shaking airstrikes
on Baghdad
by American forces,
I cursed America, I accused America
of all those bombings,
of all the relentless, ghastly assaults.

But America is a country of many good friends of mine.
America is a country where I got a college education,
where I met many good young people and excellent professors.
America is a country of many powerful poets,
great novelists and dramatists.
America is the country where I was mesmerized by the beauty
of English as spoken by Paul Robeson's "Othello."
America is the country of many good, friendly people.
America is the Golden Gate Bridge.
America is the Mississippi River.
America is the Statue of Liberty.
America is the Metropolitan Museum of Art.
America is the Empire State Building.
America is the beautiful music at Christmas time.
America is the Rockets of the Radio City Music Hall.
America is the Grand Canyon.
America is Beale Street, Memphis, Tennessee.
America is Disneyland.
America is Yankee Stadium.

Pulled by two opposing things—
many wonderful things
and the violent, bloody, heartless war started by Bush—
my heart is helplessly torn apart.

SECTION 8

A NEW YEAR SONG OF THE HORSE

—*Written on the first day of the Year of the Horse, 1990*—

Long before the car was invented,
I carried man from Mongolia to Spain,
from Alaska as far down as Cape Horn.

The dog has been only his pet,
waggling his tail, asking for a pat on the head,
or a bone of a lamb.

Of course, he is of some help,
retrieving a pheasant in a hunt,
or barking at a sneaking thief.

I am man's greatest helper,
plowing his fields,
carrying his sacks of grain, or anything heavy.

I was his comrade-in-arms,
pulling the cannon, or charging at his enemy.
I even died by his side.

Long before the plane was invented,
I could even fly over the prairie,
madly dashing with all my might,

kicking the ground with my powerful hoofs,
making him feel the thrill of speed,
he clinging to my back.

Nothing makes him so wild
as the excitement at my race,
huge crowds roaring louder than in the ballpark.

A NEW YEAR SONG OF THE SHEEP

—Written on the first day of the Year of the Sheep, 1991—

Don't call me "sheepish."
I am only meek.
I can climb
the steepest mountainsides
of the Andes,
where the air is thin and cold,
where even mountain cats dare not climb.
I occasionally bump my head
against the granite rocks
along my trail
to toughen the whole system
of my bones.
I've fed humans
with my milk, cheese and butter
in the valleys of the Euphrates,
at the foot of Mt. Olympus,
on the highlands of Mongolia.
I've clothed humans
with my thick, warm fleece
against the coldest weather.
I've even fed them
with my own flesh.
For all this,
they now sprinkle dirty stuff
over the grass I eat,
and they now let acid rains fall.
When hostile human troops are deployed
against each other
over the oil wells
in the deserts,
I calmly chew my cud in the shade of date palm trees.

A NEW YEAR SONG OF THE MONKEY

—*Written on the first day of the Year of the Monkey, 1992*—

We see glorious sunrises
from the top branches of the tallest trees,
not the merciless killings,
shootings,
bombings of humans against humans
on TV.

We hear the music of birds
singing the joy of living in the woods and plains,
not the talks
about sexual harassment,
smoking,
alcoholism,
drugs and AIDS.

We don't speak the way you humans do,
but we do scream
against your infiltration into our woods,
against your destruction of our rain forests.
We do worry
about what is happening
to some of our babies.

A NEW YEAR SONG OF THE ROOSTER

—Written on the first day of the Year of the Rooster, 1993—

Since long before the clock was invented
in the history of human civilization,
I've been a living clock for human beings,
faithfully heralding
the arrival of a new day
every morning,
telling them to wake up
and get up
and get busy gathering food.
And now this morning
I crow my loudest
in superb tenor,
telling human beings
in every corner of the world
of the arrival of my year.

A NEW YEAR SONG OF THE DOG

—Written on the first day of the Year of the Dog, 1994—

The horse has once said that I am only man's pet,
boasting of all the help
he can give.

When my master comes home,
tired out and weary,
I welcome him, waggling my tail with all my love.

I am more than a pet.
I am a friend to man,
even his best, most faithful friend.

When he has no friend, I keep him company.
I can restore his confidence,
patting his leg with my tail.

The horse says he is man's greatest helper.
But I can perform a trick
no horse can perform.

At the crowded international airport
I can sniff out any hidden cocaine
or marijuana in the smuggler's bag.

I guard my master's doorway.
too conscientious, I bite at the mailman's leg.
That's the trouble with me.

Not only his body,
I can also guard his mind,
when he is depressed, with no human friends.

A 14-LINE POEM OF THE WILD BOAR

—*Written on the 3rd day of the Year of the Wild Boar, 1995*—

My teeth I gnash
And I clash
Against my foe. I swear
Even a bear I don't fear.
With an object in my mind,
I dash, not looking behind.
With my stout snout I dig up a yam
By the side of a dam.
I leap before I look,
Jmping over a brook.
I don't care even if my enemy's build is large.
Baring my tusks sharp, I charge.
With the jet of my fart
I dart.

A NEW YEAR SONG OF THE RAT

—Written on the first day of the Year of the Rat, 1996—

Ever since human beings started to store food
in their huts,
I've lived on human food as long as I can remember.
I've snatched their grains
from their granaries.
I've stolen their cheese
from their pantries.
I've been so elusive
they can't catch me.
So they learned to use the cat
to keep their storehouses safe
from my work
as early as 4,000 years ago in Egypt.
The cat is so sly in stalking me
from behind, making no sound
on his soft-padded paws.
Human beings blame me.
They hate me.
They curse me.
They try every device to catch me.
But what do they do among themselves?
They hurt each other
with greed and arrogance,
with trickery and betrayal.
They even kill each other
with hatred and terrorism.
They use their brains
to device destructive weapons,
even blowing up an innocent atoll
in the South Pacific.

A NEW YEAR SONG OF THE COW

—Written on the first day of the Year of the Cow, 1997—

The horse says he is the greatest helper to man.
The dog says he is man's best, most faithful friend.
As for me, I am the builder of human bodies.
I have given my warm, rich milk to human babies and adults alike
all over the world ever since the dawn of human history.
More human babies feed on my milk
than on their own mothers' breast milk.
My swollen udder has been the unlimited source
of their vital nutrition.
Butter is made of my milk
Cheese is made of my milk.
Yogurt is made of my warm, rich milk
There is no such thing as a cow racetrack,
for I don't run as fast as the horse.
But, some human beings ruin their lives,
betting on horses at the racetrack.
I can't help man like the seeing eye dog.
But I am the builder of human bodies.
Human bones are made of the calcium in my milk.
And my husband, Mr. Bull is the center of attention
on New Year holidays, fighting the most exciting bull fight
on an island named "Tokunoshima"
between mainland Japan and Okinawa.

A NEW YEAR SONG OF THE TIGER

—Written on the first day of the Year of the Tiger, 1998—

What better poem can be written about me
than the one written by the noted poet
named William Blake?
I do believe it's the most splendid poem
that has ever been written about me,
so there's no need for another poem
in praise of me.
But today I will sing a song about myself,
since this is the Year of the Tiger myself.
Of all the twelve zodiacal animals of the Orient,
nay, of all the animals on Earth,
I am the most powerful, the strongest,
and the most gracefully beautiful.
What other animal has such beautiful fur as mine,
shining gold with pitch-dark stripes?
When I hunt a deer in the marshland
of the subcontinent of India,
my paws are the swiftest of all,
and my sharp claws rip the sleek sides of my prey.
My jaws crush the neck bones of a wild boar
in the rain forest of Sumatra.
When I stroll in the woods of Siberia,
I'm the most sagacious, most dignified philosopher.
When I roar at my utmost,
crouching on the granite rib of a mountain,
the whole world trembles.
And now, at the beginning of my year,
I will roar my fiercest, most resounding roar
to the whole world,
and devour the ills of humanity,
human greed for power and wealth,
the human folly in destroying the precious woods
and rain forests, my territories, my home.

A NEW YEAR SONG OF THE HARE

—Written on the first day of the Year of the Rabbit, 1999—

Of all the twelve animals
of the Oriental calendar,
I am the meekest, the swiftest-footed.
My cousin, the House Rabbit lives
in the yard of Man's home protected.

As for me, I live
in the wild full of dangers.
The House Rabbit's babies are helpless,
stark-naked, red-skinned, without fur,
blind with their eyes closed,
while my babies are ready to walk and run,
with their innocent eyes wide open,
the day they are born.
When our archenemy the Fox comes around,
I stamp hard my hind legs
to warn my little ones about the danger
in this risky world,
to let them sit dead still, holding their breath.
Then, I leap up high in the air
out of the grass,
flaunting my bright, white tail,
to draw the Fox's attention.
Taking notice of my white, fluffy tail,
he begins to chase me all at once.
I run away from my burrow,
luring the Fox to come after me.
I can outsmart him,
I can outrun him,
running all around the sunny hillside,
then back to my babies in the burrow safe.

(Note: I thought the Hare's song would be more interesting than the Rabbit's.)

A NEW YEAR SONG OF THE DRAGON

—Written on the first day of the Year of the Dragon, 2000—

Of all the twelve zodiacal animals of the Orient
I am the only one that was conceived and grew
in the womb of human imagination
and was born
into the world of harsh reality.
I have mighty jaws,
sharp, crooked claws,
powerful tail, pointed horns,
thick, straight, long whiskers,
and red, red glaring eyes.

I sometimes sit on top of the rainbow,
scanning the horizon and the sky.
I soar to the highest,
riding on the black turbulent clouds of a tornado.
I climb the Himalayas,
catching on to the icecap with my crooked claws.
I lick the permanent snow with my burning tongue,
quenching my unquenchable thirst.
I swim my way through the high seas,
raising a cloud of spray with my tail.

My hand-to-hand combat with the Tiger
is most heroic and legendary.
My might jaws clash against his,
my sharp claws scratch his beautiful fur,
his powerful paws strike my sides,
my tail swishes through the air
to hit his muscular body.
We act out a most heroic fight.

But on happy festivals, I gently alight
on the streets of Chinatown
of San Francisco,
of Yokohama,
of New York,
on the streets of Beijing,
of Hong Kong,
of Singapore,
and many other cities on Earth,
chanting,
dancing,
wading through the crowds of human beings.
I smile at the kids,
though they are a bit afraid of my fierce eyes.

Today
on the first day of my year,
the year 2000,
I make my New Year resolutions:
I will stop fighting with the Tiger
for the peace of the world.
I will inspire hopes
in the hearts
of human beings baffled by problems
by showing them my wild, gallant flight
 in the sky.

A NEW YEAR SONG OF THE SNAKE

—Written on the first day of the Year of the Snake, 2001—

My name is "Habu,"
the most ferocious poison snake
in the Amami Islands,
nay, in the whole world.
Of all the twelve animals
of the Oriental calendar
I compete with the Rat for ugliness.
I believe I'm the uglier by far.
I compete with the Monkey for wickedness.
I believe I'm the more wicked by far.
Let the whole world hate me
for my ugliness and wickedness.
I'll live my life according to my own philosophy.
My red forked sensitive tongue
slips in and out of my cold mouth,
uncannily dancing in the air,
feeling for the body temperature of my enemy.
When I detect the enemy
I coil in a flash,
getting ready to strike
with an intense hatred that seethes
in my cold-blooded heart.
I sink my sharp crooked fangs deep
into my enemy's muscular tissue
and securely inject my pent-up poison
from my swollen glands.
What a wonderful feeling!
Today, on the first day of the year,
I will strip myself of all the 20th century skin
and slither off
into time and space
of the New Century.

A NEW YEAR SONG OF THE HORSE

—Written on the first day of the Year of the Horse, 2002—

As I get set
at the starting gate,
I can feel some strange sound wave
in the roars
of human beings
ever since that September 11.
I can feel something is different
in the whole atmosphere
of my racetrack.
Something has definitely changed
in some way,
though I cannot say
exactly what has changed
in what manner,
but something has changed,
in the way human beings purchase tickets at the gate,
in the way they roar,
in the way they cry,
in the way they whistle,
at the racetrack.
Now, in this changed world
what should I do?
I would just keep my old way
by galloping
as madly as I can,
kicking the ground,
scraping the turf,
with all my powerful hoofs.

(As illustrated in *Poems of the World*)

A NEW YEAR SONG OF THE SHEEP

—Written at the beginning of the Year of the Sheep, 2003—

I eat grass in the fields.
Then I sit
in the shades of trees,
and chew my cud.
I don't eat meat like the tiger,
or the wolf.
The wild boar eats many different things.
He eats not only potatoes, melons, chestnuts, cabbages,
but also rats and snakes.
I don't do that.
The rat too eats many different things.
He steals grains and cheese
from human beings' storerooms.
All I eat is grass.
Eating grass, I make bones, muscles, milk, fat, and energy
and I also make warm, soft fleece.
Since ancient times, I have given my delicious flesh,
my rich milk,
and my warm, soft fleece
to human beings.
I don't attack, kill and eat other animals as many beasts do.
I am gentle.
I'm not greedy.
I don't crave for power.
My gentleness is as soft as my fleece.

A NEW YEAR SONG OF THE MONKEY

—Written on the first day of the Year of the Monkey, 2004—

You might have seen how we wild monkeys fight.
You say we look fierce and agile and bright.
When we fight, we bite the foe with our jaws,
and scratch the other fellow's fur with claws.
We know not how to use a stone or a stick.
We don't hit with a piece of a broken brick.
But look how shrewdly human beings fight.
They are smart, clever, crafty, wise and bright.
At the beginning of their history,
they would just fight with their fists only.
Then they learned how to use a stone and a stick.
Then they made vicious weapons that make us sick,
weapons that fly and pierce and explode and kill.
Just look how they beat their foe to their fill.
They even devised something horrendous.
Its destructive power is tremendous.
Hundreds of thousands of their own species,
in a flash, could be turned into charred pieces
with their most, violent, destructive device.
"Don't be arrogant!" is my keen advice
to the smartest creature on the Planet.
"Your arrogance will catch you in the net."

A NEW YEAR SONG OF THE ROOSTER

—Written on the first day of the Year of the Rooster, 2005—

In my first cockcrow
of this New Year's Day morning
of my year,
I flap my powerful wings
and sing of the dawn,
heralding the arrival of my year.
I loudly announce my wish
to make the year 2005
a year of songs,
a year of hopes,
a year of dreams.

In my second cockcrow
of this New Year's Day morning
of my year,
I flap my vibrant wings
and sing of the joy
of being alive,
the joy of strutting, and running,
the joy of watching flowers, and the moon and stars.

In my third cockcrow
of this New Year's Day morning
of my year,
I flap my ambitious wings
and sing out my prayer loud,
for world peace,
in my superb, splendid tenor,
for an end of the unstable situation
in that Middle Eastern country.

A NEW YEAR SONG OF THE DOG

—Written on the first day of the Year of the Dog, 2006—

On the morning of New Year's Day
of the year of the Dog,
that is my year,
I run out
into the wilderness
and bark my first bark of the year.

On the morning of New Year's Day
of the year of the Dog,
that is my year,
I run out
into the wilderness
and greet the bright first morning sun of the year.

On the morning of New Year's Day
of the year of the Dog,
that is my year,
I run out
into the wilderness
and breathe in the fresh morning air
deep into my robust lungs.

Then, as I breather it out,
I sing the happy, happy New Year song
with all my heart, mind, soul and might,
the song full of hope, joy and delight.

A NEW YEAR SONG OF THE WILD BOAR

—*Written on the first day of the Year of the Wild Boar, 2007*—

I shiver with cold these winter mornings.
But this is the bright New Year's Day morning
Of my year in the lunar calendar.
Early this morning I get up and dash
Straight to the summit of the tall mountain
To greet the bright, wondrous New Year's Day sun.
Like my friend, Hare, I'm good at running uphill.
Brother Pig lives in an apartment
Built by Man, and is fed by him every day.
I seek and find and get my own food
In the woods, on the hills, and in the mountains.
This morning I sing a song of myself
With all my rough brown bristles up,
Looking down at the human village below.
It's wonderful to see the bright sun rise
In the clear, eastern New Year's Day sky.
I am 12 years older today
Than when I sang my "Song of the Wild Boar"
Last on the New Year's Day morning of my year, 1995.
My tusks are more yellowish now than before,
But they are sharp enough to hit my foe.
My snout is a wee bit thinner than before,
But still tough enough to dig up yams,
Lily bulbs in woods, potatoes on a farm.
My teeth are a little looser than before,
But strong enough to crunch and crush acorns,
Chestnuts, walnuts in the hush of night.
We, wild boars are reckless, dauntless fighters,
But we have no such things as wars or weapons.
And we have no such things as god or creed
That would sharply divide us into sects,
Filling our hearts with stark hostility.

A NEW YEAR SONG OF THE RAT

—Written on the first day of the Year of the Rat, 2008—

Ever since I was born on this Planet,
I have been a thief,
a talented thief,
a most professional thief,
ever stealing food from Man's storeroom,
his pantry, paddy fields, and fruit farms.
I've often stolen cheese from his kitchen
in the dark of night.
I bite his sugarcane in the daytime.
I munch his sweet potatoes at night.
I eat what he eats.
I like what he likes.
He tries to catch me with the rattrap.
But, I'm so smart that I don't get easily caught.
Anyway I steal what I eat.
But look, what do human beings do?
They are hell-bent on getting more than they can eat.
They even sail far out to the other side of the Planet
to catch tuna fish they like.
They never hesitate to invade other lands
to expand their sphere of influence.
We rats fight with our jaws and paws,
but human beings devise horrible weapons
to kill other members of their own species.
They destroy forests to raise corn and oil palms
just to make fuel for their cars.
They do anything to make more money.
They do anything to indulge themselves in pleasure.
They do anything to have power over others.
They don't stop emitting huge amounts of CO_2,
thus making our Planet ever warmer,
raising sea level all over our Planet.

A NEW YEAR SONG OF THE COW

—Written on the first day of the Year of the Cow, 2009—

I greet the dawn of my year with a happy heart,
while the human world is full of troubles
violent conflicts in different parts of the Planet,
the once-in-hundred-year financial crisis,
the ever worsening global warming.

When the mechanism of economy isn't working right,
when hopes of human beings are dwindling,
when dreams of human beings are withering,
when human babies are crying with hunger,
my udder is full, almost bursting with rich milk.
I'll give them my nutritious milk as much as I can.

When human beings are troubled with problems,
I chew my cud
in the shade of trees
as gently as my dear friend Sheep.

What's all this fuss about the human world?
I'll keep my temper at ease,
just like my gentle-hearted friend Sheep,
ever changing the grass I eat into rich, nutritious milk
for the worried, hungry human beings.

A NEW YEAR SONG OF THE TIGER
—Written on the first day of the Year of the Tiger, 2010—

At the dawn of the first day
of the first month of the Year of the Tiger, 2010
I look all over the world,
from the east to the west,
from the south to the north.

And I inhale all the fresh air of the New Year's Day morning
deep into my powerful lungs
and roar my first roar of the year
as far as the end
of the endless universe.

A man in ancient China said,
"The tiger leaves its fur after death,
and man leaves his name after death."
But, I don't really leave my fur after death.
Sure, not all men leave their names after death.
Some leave noble names.
Some leave ignoble names.
But, most of them die nameless, humble, silent.

But, when I look at the human world
full of arrogance, greed, distrust and conflicts,
I gnash my angry fangs,
and sharpen my mighty claws,
scratching a fine pine tree's trunk
or a gray granite rock.
And I warn them, roaring as loudly as I can,
"Unless you become wise enough
to get rid of the terrible weapons your clever minds have invented,
you will leave nothing but the ruins of what your hands have built,
your charred black skeletons and scorched forests.
Your songs, artworks, books, even your dreams will be gone."

THE TIGER'S ADVICE TO MAN

—Written on the 3rd Day of the Year of the Tiger, 2010—

Sure it's foolish to fight among yourselves
and it's crazy to explode yourself
with explosives strapped around your belly.
It's foolish to start a war of invasion
into another country.
You should stop being foolish and crazy.
You should all stand up and sing and dance.
Why don't you call the Octopus
out of his hole in the coral reef
this glorious New Year's Day morning
of my year
and ask him to teach you
how to dance his "Octopus Dance"?
Stop wasting your lives, fighting, wrangling,
hating, arguing, and screaming.
You should all stand up and sing and dance
on this glorious morning
on my year,
the great Year of the Tiger.
That's the best way to live your life.
That's the best way to enjoy your life.

(As illustrated in *Poems of the World*)

A NEW YEAR SONG OF THE RABBIT

—Written on the first day of the Year of the Rabbit, 2011—

The year 2011 is my year,
the Year of the Rabbit.

I remember
the year 2010 was the Year of the Tiger.
So, on the morning of the New Year's Day
of the Year of the Tiger,
he roared his first roar of the year
with all his utmost power
as far as the end
of the endless universe.

(As illustrated in *Poems of the World*)

I, the Rabbit, don't roar,
nor do I sing.
All I can do is just run and jump and dance.

So, on the morning
of the New Year's Day of my year,
I run and dash and dart
with my powerful hind legs
to the top of the hill
to greet the New Year's Day sunrise of my year.

And there on the top of the hill,
I leap up
three times
into the cool New Year's Day sky.

Then, I dance my lively
dance with all my might.
Everyone enjoys watching me dance my lively dance,
the most lively dance
in the whole world.

A NEW YEAR SONG OF THE DRAGON

—Written on the first day of the Year of the Dragon, 2012—

The year 2011 was the Year of the Rabbit,
the gentlest of all the twelve zodiacal animals
 in the Orient's traditional calendar.
However, his year was full of terrible happenings,
the Great East Japan Earthquake of March 11,
one of the strongest in history,
triggering one of the most destructive tsunamis in history,
which in turn triggered disasters at the nuclear power plant,
the worst nuclear disasters in history,
contaminating the air, land, and sea.
How I wish I could show human beings how to handle troubles
at their nuclear power plants!
They should stop stealing energy
from the nucleus of the atom of uranium
by breaking it so arrogantly and so selfishly.
Now, on the morning of the New Year's Day
of the Year of the Dragon,
I alight on the crest of Mt. Fuji
and pray, gazing on the New Year's Day sun,
for the peace and weal of the entire world.
On this beautiful morning of New Year's Day
 I will fully enjoy Japanese *sake*,
forgetting all about the troubles of the past year
and think of the schedule of my dance performance for this year.
When the Chinese Spring Festival comes around,
I'll wade across the vast Pacific,
propelling myself with my powerful tail,
raising enormous clouds of spray,
projecting countless colorful rainbows
all over the islands of Hawaii on my way,
and land on San Francisco.
Then I will go to the Chinatown there and
dance my Dragon dance,
making all the people happy and merry.

(As illustrated in *Poems of the World*)

A NEW YEAR SONG OF THE SNAKE

—Written on the first day of the Year of the Snake, 2013—

Of all the twelve animals
of the Oriental calendar,
I am the ugliest,
the most loathsome to see.
No one likes me,
because they abhor my long, cold, creeping body.
Everyone gives me a hateful look,
so I slither along all by myself in the wet grassland.

I have a cousin named "Habu"
in the Ryukyu Islands between mainland Japan and Taiwan.
He is the most dreaded poison snake in the world.
Hiding in trees or grasses,
his sensitive tongue can feel his enemy's body temperature.
He will attack even a human or a cow.

I have another cousin named "Python."
Huge and powerful, he can choke even a leopard or a man
by tightly winding his long, cold body around his prey.
Python's skin has a beautiful pattern.
His skin is highly valued in making "snakeskin samisens,"
but now snakeskin is artificially produced
in order to save my cousin, Python.
The people in the Ryukyu Islands happily play "snakeskin samisens,"
providing music for their lively island dances
at the seaside village common under the moon.

And now, as I lick the delicious Japanese *sake*
with my forked tongue on this beautiful New Year's Day morning
of my year, the Year of the Snake,
I begin to feel happy.
No matter how ugly and loathsome I may look,
I feel most grateful to be alive. "Happy New Year!"

A NEW YEAR SONG OF THE HORSE

—Written on the first day of the Year of the Horse, 2014—

I am the fastest runner
Of all the twelve animals
Of the Oriental calendar.
I can run faster than the Rabbit.
I can run faster than the Wild Boar.
I can run even faster than the Tiger.
I can make Man go wild with excitement at my racetrack.
Now, on the morning of New Year's Day on my year
I gallop to the top of the highest hill
To greet the New Year's Day sun,
Since it's my custom on New Year's Day morning
To greet the first sunrise of the year.
It's great to see the sun gloriously rise out of the immense Pacific Ocean.
I kick hard the dirt of the ground,
Making the rhythmic sound with my robust hoofs
All along the road. There on the hilltop
I inhale the freshest air of the year
Deep into my powerful lungs
And loudly neigh my first neigh of the year
Toward every corner of the world,
Declaring my big "Nay!" to Man's conflicting world.
The cool morning air
Feels pleasant on my sleek, brown, beautiful fur.
The bulging muscles of my legs and shoulders are almost bursting
With power.
There on the hilltop
I pray God to help Man solve his conflicts on Earth.
I pray God to lead Man to abolish all his nuclear weapons on Earth.
I pray God to teach Man to decommission all his nuclear plants on Earth.
And now, I begin to gallop into the year 2014
With my heart full of bright hopes.

A NEW YEAR SONG OF THE SHEEP

—Written on the first day of the Year of the Sheep, 2015—

It was twelve years ago today, in 2003, that I sang a New Year song
For the Year of the Sheep,
And another Year of the Sheep has come around.
We, Sheep, feed on green grass,
Transforming it into pure white rich milk,
White soft fleece,
And red, juicy, delicious meat
For human beings.
The Mongolian nomads have kept us, Sheep,
In their wide, vast prairies and highlands
Ever since time immemorial.
Even small kids there lead us to green grasslands
And help their fathers keep us safe from hungry Wolves,
Deftly riding on their stout, strong Horses
Under the clear, blue Mongolian skies.
Our contribution to human life has been immense,
Not only in Mongolia,
But also in both Americas,
In Australia and New Zealand.
Now, looking at the conflicts and violence in the human world,
I firmly believe that the human beings should learn from us, Sheep,
How to live gently, and peacefully.
We don't fight like human beings.
We don't kill and eat other animals like Tigers or Wolves, either.
And now we see some grasslands dwindling
Due to human activities.
Human beings should try to keep the beautiful Planet Earth safe
For all the living things,
Nay, not only for all the living things,
But also for all the beautiful mountains, rivers,
Deserts, seas, and skies.
—This is my New Year wish for the year 2015.—

(As illustrated in *Poems of the World*)

A NEW YEAR SONG OF THE MONKEY

—Written on the first day of the Year of the Monkey, 2016—

I heartily enjoy looking at this glorious sunrise
in the New Year's Day morning of my year,
comfortably sitting on the tallest tree's topmost branch.
The year 2015 was the Year of the Sheep,
the most gentle, the most peace-loving animal of all, but the most violent terrorist attacks occurred
in the most beautiful city of Europe. On the night of November 13
some people were enjoying music in a concert hall
and some other people were enjoying their dinner at cafes.
And then, those terrorists started shooting
at innocent human beings indiscriminately.
And I should also mention that we monkeys can't draw any pictures,
not to mention a caricature of a prophet.
Human beings shouldn't abuse their freedom of expression
and insult other human beings' faith.
There are enough subjects to satirize in the world.
We monkeys just can't understand such human activities.
We monkeys don't kill others indiscriminately,
nor do we draw any caricatures to insult the other side's faith.
We monkeys don't do "monkey business."
It's human beings that do "monkey business."
Some human beings dub others "mimic monkeys,"
as if we monkeys are imitators.
It's human beings that make and sell imitations.
We don't use a rock or a stick when we fight.
We just use our fists and jaws.
Human brains were clever enough to invent the most heinous bombs,
and they were even foolish enough to use them some 70 years ago.
Now, they should become wise enough to abolish them.
I hope all the human beings will get together in 2016
and start working together to build a safe, sane, and secure world.

A NEW YEAR SONG OF THE ROOSTER

—Written for New Year's Day of the Year of the Rooster, 2017—

For my first cockcrow
Of this New Year's Day morning of my year,
I joyfully flap my powerful wings
And sing of the wonder
Of being alive,
The joy of welcoming the New Year.

For my second cockcrow
Of this New Year's Day morning of my year,
I joyfully flap my vibrant wings
And sing a song
In praise of my wife, Mrs. Hen
For laying so many eggs,
The vital ingredient for many, nutrient delicacies.

(As illustrated in *Poems of the World*)

For my third cockcrow
Of this New Year's Day morning of my year,
I joyfully flap my ambitious wings,
And sing out my sincere prayer
For world peace,
For phasing out of human beings' terrible acts of terrorism,
For mutual understanding among all the human beings on Earth.

My cousins, brown-red gamecocks bravely fight only for a prize.
They never kill each other like human beings.
I earnestly hope that human beings will realize some day
That no other animals on Earth kill each other so heartlessly.

A NEW YEAR SONG OF THE DOG

—Written for the Year of the Dog, 2018—

At the beginning
Of the Year of the Dog,
I reverentially greet the glorious New Year sunrise,
Looking back on the Year of the Rooster that has just gone by,
And think of what will be in store for my year.

The prospect of peace
In the human world seems rather dark
With all the conflicts, distrust and terrorism,
But I'll bark
My first, loudest bark of the year
In the park
With all the power of my strong throat
And bring a spark
Of hope into human hearts,
Reminding them of the foolishness of fighting,
Reminding them of the merit
Of turning the gray deserts
Into green grasslands
With the fresh water of friendly cooperation,
Where will sing many a lark
For the good of all the living things,
And let the human beings listen
To the beautiful music of Bach.

(An illustration taken from *Poems of the World*)

SECTION 9

CHAUCER ABOARD A SPACESHIP

Throgh the erephone in my helmet
I koude here the countedoun
Neerynge zero, "fyve—foure—three—,"
Whyles I heeld my breeth ful tense.

Thanne, right anon as I herde
The word, "Ignicioun!," the hool shippe shook,
Rorynge sodeynly, and bigan to sore faste
Up and up to the cenyth of the skye.

Throgh the periscope I koude espie
The orisonte of the Atlantyk turnynge
Rounde and rounde, as up sored the rokkete
Muche faster than the fastest bullete.

I have now goon into grete orbyt
Withinne fyve minutes after blaste-of,
Now dryvynge the spaceshippe with myn owene honde,
Lookynge doun upon the blew erthe rounde.

Oh, ful wondirful is this space flyghte,
Circlynge rounde the grete erthe,
Saylynge among the sterres bryghte
Of the univers that hath no ende.

CHAUCER AT CAPE KENNEDY

On the launchynge pad, the talle spaceshippe stondeth,
Pointynge its nose to the cenyth of the skye.
Oh, it almost recheth the hevene hye,
Stikynge up heigh over the fogge that hovereth.

As the countedoun proceedeth seconde by seconde,
The brighte rede sonne bigynneth to rysen
Up the orisonte of the wyde, blew Atlantyk Occian,
Sheddynge morwenynge lighte al over the londe.

Now, as the countedoun nereth zero,
The pulse of everychoon's herte bigynneth to
Hoppe and lepe ful faste mo and mo,
Thynkynge of the aventure of the hero.

Thanne, sodeynly the super-stronge
Saturne engynes begynnen to sterte,
Shakynge the talle, shynynge spaceshippe smerte,
Belchynge furyus flaumes, rede, yelwe, and orange.

As everychoon looketh up, on toos stondynge,
Strecchynge his or her nekke longe and heighe,
The spaceshippe shooteth into the sterres of the skye,
Shakynge off the erthe's pulle, like thonders rorynge.

CHAUCER ENJOYS *RICHARD III* IN TOKYO

I jolily crossed,
   Nat the Thames over to Southwerk,
     But the stremes of peple and bisy cars
       In the twentieth century Tokyo.

I entered,
   Nat the gate of a thatched medieval theatre,
     But the byg facade
       Of a super-moderne structor.

I saugh,
   Nat oure Burbage, Will Kemp, ne Olivier ther,
     But Japane's Kabuky actour, Kanzaburo
       Pleyynge the role of Richard III.

Was Burbage hymself as goode
   As this Kanzaburo's Gloucesteer?
     A Japanese actresse waylynge, faire, and finally wonne,
       Was as reel and eek as trewe as Anne.

Thogh I herde the pleyeres speke
   Nat the speche of oure Engelond,
     I was ful astoned
       By the spirit that was Shakespeere's.

Thus, oure Bard lyveth on
   Foure centuries latter
     In the hertes, blood, and speche
       Of those actours of the Fer Est also.

CHAUCER AT LEICESTER SQUARE

Whan that colde wyndes of Januarie bigonne
To blowen in the londe of Britaign,
Publyc servyce werkeris alle seyden,
"No heyere paye, No werke!" and makeden
A decisioun not to werke in hospitales,
Ambulaunce servyce, and scoles.
Garbagemen refused to collecten
Garbage from the stretes and bigonne to sitten
At hoom, or heedquarters of their uniounes,
So, ech of the stretes of citees, and tounes,
Specially of Londoun, is a horrible sighte.
And I am astoned at the heighte
Of pyles of plastyc sakkes of garbage,
And rattes crawlen out of the sewage
Right into the stretes, up the moundes of swille.
They clymben and eten on their owene wille.
Whan that I walke a Londoun strete at nyght,
The strete lyghtes seme not halfe as bright
As the eyen of the rattes grete
That shynen from moundes by the syde of the strete.
I knowe not which hath caused this ailmente,
Tightnesse of Callaghan's gouvernmente
Or publyc servyce werkeris' stubbornnesse.
But one thyng I knowe: bothe sydes neden moderatenesse,
Nat stubbornnesse, and the longe stryke
Maketh everychon at herte very sike.

(*Mainichi Daily News*, February 25, 1979)

CHAUCER AT THE 50TH REUNION
—Written for Alumni Day, 2004—

Whan that the gay monthe of Juyn hath dressed
The maple tres in fresshe, bright grene
Alonge Western Avenue in Albanye,
And pansyes, tulippes, and roses, whyte and reede,
Blosmen and dauncen to the swete songes
Of briddes on treetolppes in Washingtoun Park,
Manye Bluejayes comen with ful glad hertes
From every countee's ende of the Empyre State,
Neweburgh, Mideltoun, Yonkeres, Troye,
Bynghamtoun, Elmyra, Grete Nekke,
And Newe Yorke, the greteste, bisyest citee
In the world, ay, from manye oother tounes
Of Newe Yorke State they comen to Albanye
For to attenden their 50th reunioun.
As they now meeten and talken togidre loude
With muche feelynge and with wyde smyles,
Pattynge ech oother's shuldre goode and hard,
They thynken bak on their collegge dayes
Of moore than 50 yeres agoo,
Their happy collegge dayes at Albanye State
Whan their hertes weren yonge, chekes rosy;
They thynken of their deere, olde, worthy professores;
Ay, they remembre how Minerva smyled,
Lookynge doun upon hem whan they gatt
An "F" in the test of Frenssh or Psychologye;
They thynken of ice-cremes of Brubacheer Halle;
And they thynken of manye pleyes they have sene
In their deere, olde Page Halle,
Specially the delitable "Silver Corde"
That their classe's pleyer, John Layng, was in.

SECTION 10

Poems Translated into Other Languages

A Chinese translation
My Grandfather
我的祖父

我的祖父
活到九十四周岁,常年
住在海岛
他的肩膀宽阔
手臂健硕
骑着马

在烤焦海岛的阳光下
半裸着被太阳晒黑的身躯
耕种他在山上
坚硬、遍布岩石的小块农田
他的心中没有猛烈的台风
早逝亲人的死也没能把他压垮
那些亲人已经安息
在我们的家族墓地
那山脚下
距今已经三十多年

但他会跳起那消瘦的脚
跺着
举起他骨瘦如柴的手臂
咬紧他没牙的下巴
自黑色眼眸的深处
凝视着我
同时用他无言的嘴
发出吼叫和唾弃
几近疯狂

若他见我偷偷溜走
像个胆怯的傻瓜
在尘世的角落
　害怕人群
　害怕风和冰雹……

（樱娘 译）

A French translation of a tanka

アフリカの猿々たち山で笑っている殺し合いしてる人間を見て

les babouins
dans les montagnes d'Afrique
rient
à regarder les êtres humains
s'entretuer

afurika no hihitachi yama de waratte iru koroshiai shiteru ningen o mite

The dog apes / of Africa are laughing / in the mountains,
looking at human beings / killing each other

Naoki Koriyama
"No More War, Please" [S'il vous plaît, fini la guerre]
International Tanka 1 2017

Cirrus n° 8 ~ octobre 2017 ~ p 45

A French translation of a tanka

新しい年はウサギの跳ねる年ウサギ の如く踊りたい年

le Nouvel An
l'année des bondissements
du Lapin, l'année
où j'aimerais danser
comme le lapin

atarashii toshi wa usagi no haneru toshi usagi no gotoku odoritaitoshi

*The New Year / is the Year of the Rabbit, / when he will jump.
Like the rabbit, I would like / to dance in the New Year*

Naoki Koriyama
"On the Wings of Tanka" [sur les ailes du tanka]
The Tanka Journal 38 2011

Cirrus n° 8 ~ octobre 2017 ~ p.40

A Greek translation of POETRY CLASS IN JAPAN

Ποιήματα του ΝΑΟΣΙ ΚΟΡΙΓΙΑΜΑ στα ελληνικά σε απόδοση της Ζαχαρούλας Γαϊτανάκη

NAOSHI KORIYAMA, Japan

POETRY CLASS IN JAPAN,

ΤΑΞΗ ΠΟΙΗΣΗΣ ΣΤΗΝ ΙΑΠΩΝΙΑ

*Ο δάσκαλος της Αγγλικής
συνοδεύει τους μαθητές του
όλη τη διαδρομή,
πάνω από αρκετές χιλιάδες μίλια,
στην εκκλησία Στοκ Πόγκες
και τους αφήνει να καθίσουν και ν' ακούσουν
τον ποιητή Τόμας Γκραίη.*

*Ο δάσκαλος της Αγγλικής
συνοδεύει τον ποιητή Τόμας Γκραίη
όλη τη διαδρομή,
πάνω από δυο εκατοντάδες χρόνια
στην τάξη των Αγγλικών
και τον αφήνει να μιλήσει
περί της ποιμαντορικής ζωής.*

An Italian translation of AT A GARDEN IN KYOTO

IN UN GIARDINO DI KYOTO
- guardando una copia da un paese lontano -

non parlare loro
solamente lasciali seduti -
seduti lì senza parlare
a lungo quanto vogliono
sulla panca di pietra
sul bordo del laghetto
dove fioriscono i gigli d'acqua
e nuota la carpa

non parlare loro
solo lascia che ascoltino
la pace
di questo laghetto
in un profondo sentire

lasciali sognare
della mente perspicace
dell'antico architetto paesaggista
che ha potuto scavare
e rubare
la bellezza
della natura
con la zappa

A Korean translation of TIME AND SPACE

郡山 直 作
李廷基 譯

時間과 空間

客船이
넓고 넓은 바다의
거대한 파도를
타고 넘으며
용감하게
항해를 계속해 나갈 때
時間이
나그네
가슴의 고동을 통하여
끊임없이 자꾸 흘러간다
나그네는
가장 윗쪽 甲板의
난간에
기대어 서서
하늘을 쳐다보고 있다
그러자 하늘에서도
몇 백만의 무수한 별들이
時間과 空間의 한복판에서
소리도 없이
여행을 계속하고 있다

A Korean translation of AN ARTIST'S APOLOGY TO HIS DAUGHTER
딸을 향한 어느 화가의 사과謝過

너의 아버지가 그린
여인의 누드그림을
볼 때
아마도 불편할 게다.
풍만한 가슴의
완만한 곡선을 재창조하느라
아버지는 그 여인들을
뚫어져라 관찰했겠지.
모델의 목덜미에 흘러내린 머리카락도
한 올 한 올 세었을 테고.
화포 위에 붓질하며
눈 앞 여인의 심장박동도
느꼈으리라.
아마도 너의 어머니보다
그 여인들을 더 사랑했으리라.
시간은 흘러가도 여기 그림 속에 여전히 여자들이 있다,
태양아래 벌거벗은 몸을
드러내 놓은 여자들이.

Translated into Korean by Rachel S. Rhee & Kyung Hwa Rhee

A Vietnamese translation of A LOAF OF POETRY

T.S. Naoshi Koriyama:

" *Bạn trộn*
bột
của kinh nghiệm
với
men
của cảm hứng
rồi nhào lộn thật kỹ
với lòng tử tế
sau đó, hãy đập mạnh
hết sức
rồi để yên
cho đến khi
bột nở lớn
bằng sức phồng bên trong
lúc đó
nhào trộn lần nữa
rồi
tạo hình
đưa vào khuôn tròn
nướng
trong lò
giữa trái tim "

About the Author

Naoshi Koriyama was born on Kikaijima in the Amami Islands which lie between mainland Japan and Okinawa 1926

Entered Kagoshima Normal School 1941, graduating from it 1947

Taught at Somachi Vocational High School on Kikaijima from October1947 to July 1948

Studied at Okinawa Foreign Language School from September 1948 to March 1949

Worked at Kadena Air Base as interpreter and then at the Ryukyu Military Government as translator from March 1949 to May 1950

Studied at the University of New Mexico 1950-51

Studied at the New York State College for Teachers at Albany 1951-1954, graduating from the college 1954, (B.A.)

Started writing poetry in English 1952

Started submitting poetry to *The Christian Science Monitor* 1954, and then to *Poetry Nippon* and *The Mainichi Daily News*

Taught English at Obirin Junior College in Tokyo 1956-1961

Taught English and poetry at Toyo University 1961-1997, retiring 1997

Attended the 5th World Congress of Poets held in San Francisco 1981

Attended the 9th Mirbad Poetry Festival held in Baghdad 1988 and also visited Babylon

Attended the World Congress of Poets in Milan 1988; in Seoul 1990; in Memphis, Tennessee 1995; in Buckinghamshire, England 1997; in Bangkok 2002; in Plainview, Texas 2004; in Taishan, China 2005; in Osaka, Japan 2013

Publications

Poetry

Coral Reefs, (Hokuseido Press, 1957)
Plum Tree in Japan and Other Poems, (Hokuseido Press, 1959)
Songs from Sagamihara, (Hokuseido Press, 1967)
By the Lakeshore and Other Poems, (Hokuseido Press,1977)
Selected Poems 1954-1985, (Hokuseido Press, 1989)
Poesie—Poems translated into Italian—, (Forum/ Quinta Generazione, Italy, 1990)
Eternal Grandeur and Other Poems, (Hokuseido Press, 1994)
Collected Poems, (Hokuseido Press, 1996)
Poems about the Iraq War and Other Poems, (Eiko-sha, 2004)
Shijin no Inryoku—Poems translated into Japanese—(Coal Sack, 2010)

Essays

Another Bridge over the Pacific, (Vantage Press, 1993)

Translations

We Wrote These Poems—Poems by Mentally Challenged Children—(Hokuseido Press, 1982)
Like Underground Water—The Poetry of Mid-Twentieth Century Japan—co-translated with Edward Lueders, (Copper Canyon Press, 1995))
Black Flower in the Sky by Chong Ki-Sheok, co-translated with Elizabeth Ogata, (Katydid Books,2000)
Beautiful Amami Island Folk Songs, (Hokuseido Press, 2001)
Burs of Chestnuts—One Hundred Tanaka—by Koichi Kansaku, (privately printed, 2002)
Pilgrimages to Old Battlegrounds by Yuko Nakatsu, (Coal Sack Publishing Company, 2010)
A Trip to Canada—100 Tanaka in 5 Languages—by Koichi Kansaku, co-translated with Michiko Asahina, Mitsuo Hori, and Xu Sanyi, (Asahi Shuppan-sha, 2011)
Soul Seeds—Revelations & Drawings—by Carolyn Mary Kleefeld, (co-published by Coal Sack Publishing Company, Tokyo and Cross-Cultural Communications, New York, 2014)
Japanese Tales from Times Past—Stories of Fantasy and Folklore from *Konjaku Monogatari Shu*—, co-translated with Bruce Allen, (Tuttle Publishing, 2015)
Doronkono Uta—Poems by Children Working with Clay—(Godo Shuppan, 2016)
The Divine Kiss—Poems and Drawings—by Carolyn Mary Kleefeld, co-published by Coal Sack Publishing Company, Tokyo and Cross-Cultural Communications, New York, 2017)

Poems Reprinted in School Textbooks

"Unfolding Bud"
Reflections on a Gift of Watermelon Pickle, (Scott, Foresman, 1966)
This Life, (Pergamon Press, Australia, 1974)
Types of Literature, (Ginn, 1981)
McDougal Littell Literature, Green Level (1982)
Galaxies I, (Addison-Wesley, Canada, 1990)
Textures,(Maskew Miller Longman, South Africa,)
Reflections on a Gift of Watermelon Pickle, 2nd Edition
Literature: Steps to Success, (MacMillan Education, Australia, 2016)

"Jetliner"
Zero Makes Me Hungry, (Lothrop, 1976)
Time Enough, (Holt, Rinehart and Winston of Canada, 1979)
Discovering Yourself, (Heath, 1981)
The World Ahead, (Ginn, 1985)
Invitations, (McGraw-Hill Ryerson, Canada, 1985)
Face to Face, (Scott Foresman, 1987)
Houghton Mifflin English, (Houghton Mifflin, 1992)
Imagine POETRY Magazine, (Prentice Hall Canada, 1993)
Prentice Hall Literature, Silver Level, (Prentice Hall, 1996)

"A loaf of poetry"
Reading Literature, Red Level, (McDougal, Littell, 1989)
Literature and Language, (McDougal, Littell, 1994)
Choices in Literature, Bronze Level, (Prentice Hall, 1997)
詩を楽しむ(*How to Enjoy Poetry*) ,(Dogakusha, Japan, 2008)

"Parting"
Rainbow Colours, (McGraw-Hill Ryerson, Canada)

"Time and Space"
Four Seasons,(City Press, 1984)
Reading Literature, Blue Level, (McDougal, Littell, 1985)

"Harvest," "Summer on the Home Island," "Time and Space"
Galaxies II, (Addison-Wesley, Canada, 1991)

A Fresh Loaf of Poetry from Japan

Copyright ©2018 by Naoshi Koriyama
All rights reserved.
No part of this publication may be reproduced, stored in a retrieval system, or transmitted in any form or by any means, electronic, mechanical, photocopying, recording, or otherwise, without the prior permission of the publisher.

Published in Japan.   ISBN978-4-86584-303-3

For information contact : BookWay
ONO KOUSOKU INSATSU CO.,LTD.
62, HIRANO-MACHI, HIMEJI-CITY, HYOGO 670-0933 JAPAN
(Phone) 079-222-5372 (Fax) 079-223-3523